BLACK GOAT BLUES

TOR BOOKS BY LEVI BLACK

Red Right Hand

Black Goat Blues

LEVI BLACK

TOR

A TOM DOHERTY ASSOCIATES BOOK
NEW YORK

BLACK GOAT BLUES

BLACK GOAT BLUES

Designed by Greg Collins

A Tor Book
Published by Tom Doherty Associates
175 Fifth Avenue
New York, NY 10010

www.tor-forge.com

Tor® is a registered trademark of Macmillan Publishing Group, LLC.

The Library of Congress Cataloging-in-Publication Data is available upon request.

ISBN 978-0-7653-8250-4 (hardcover)
ISBN 978-1-4668-8761-9 (ebook)

Our books may be purchased in bulk for promotional, educational, or business use. Please contact your local bookseller or the Macmillan Corporate and Premium Sales Department at 1-800-221-7945, extension 5442, or by email at MacmillanSpecialMarkets@macmillan.com.

First Edition: November 2017

Printed in the United States of America

0 9 8 7 6 5 4 3 2 1

DEDICATED TO THE MISSUS, AS ALWAYS

ACKNOWLEDGMENTS

Ah, books. Slippery little beasts they are, hard to corral. To get this one in the barn required a few folks.

Lucienne Diver: Always sublime and superb.

Greg Cox: Hitting the target like a marksman with the edits. Truly a pleasure to work with.

The Tor team: Rocking the publishing game without compare.

The Missus: As always, you keep me moving.

All the folks who bought, reviewed, supported, and cheered for *Red Right Hand* and my turn at the wheel.

Thank you all.

BLACK GOAT BLUES

1

—————————

DARKNESS PRESSES AGAINST the windows of the car. It's not my car, just one that somebody left unlocked. I needed to sit for a moment after wishing myself here. Using magick can really suck the batteries dry.

Here is Arizona. I'm assuming anyway. Most of the license plates on the cars in this lot are Arizona. I'm no detective but seems like a good sign that I'm in the "Grand Canyon State." Through the windshield I can see people in the lake of neon light thrown off the sign for the bar. They walk in twos and threes and tens, most of them laughing or talking. The ones going in move with purpose against the chill of the night air. The ones leaving are more aimless, some actually stumbling, the cold held at bay by the alcohol in their bloodstream.

It's a country-and-western bar, DOC HOLLIDAY's sprawling across the front of the place in swooping neon letters next to a ten-foot-tall backlit sign of a cowboy in a long coat. It's a big, gaudy, *public* place. The kind of place I try to avoid now.

But the thing I'm hunting is in there.

So I *will* be going in.

Soon.

Soon, I said.

My thumb swipes the phone screen and it flares to life so bright I have to blink. Scroll call list and hit the button and the phone is ringing on the other end.

"Hey." The voice that answers is warm and a little raspy. I woke him up.

"Hey, Lionel," I say.

"No change in John. He's still the same." I've trained Lionel to not waste time on small talk. By *John* he means John Doe and that's Daniel, my . . . someone I care about a lot.

Shit, wait.

Someone I *love* a lot.

"I know. I'm just checking in."

"Are you going to come see him anytime soon?"

"Soon as I can, Lionel." It's been almost a month. "Anyone by to visit?"

"Only us at the hospital."

Something inside me unclenches. "Good." If Daniel is still off the books then he's still safe. And it lets me know the magick I used on the administration to make him that way is still holding.

"If we knew his name we could contact—"

"Not going to happen, Lionel."

"But—"

"Do we have to play this game again?"

"Can't blame me for trying."

"Don't be so sure of that."

Silence grows on the phone, but I don't want to say anything or hang up.

From the seat beside me comes a rustling sound and I feel the soft brush of fabric against my arm.

Fine. Okay. Fine. I'm coming.

"I've got to go."

"Okay," Lionel says. "Call and be cryptic and vague anytime."

"Take care of him."

"I have been." There's an edge to his words.

"It's appreciated."

"Hey, Jane?" Lionel doesn't know my real name either.

"Yeah?" I know what's coming.

"Take care of *yourself*."

I hang up.

Yeah, right, Lionel. Where's the fun in that?

I take a deep breath and step out of the car. The wind kicks, cutting through my thin T-shirt. It's freezing. I thought Arizona was supposed to be hot, but the air bites and the metal collar, the torc given to me by a fallen love goddess, the thing that allows me to wish myself places, around my throat goes cold against my skin. I hold my hand out and a darkness slithers across the seats, sliding over my arm and around my body. I shrug into it and it shifts and adjusts against me until it becomes a long black coat, still tattered on its edges but mostly healed. The chill is cut off sharply. As the coat settles, a soft alien song begins to trill at the edge of my mind.

The coat is eager, ready to go.

I try to let some of its enthusiasm infect me.

The effort makes me say aloud to it: "Don't get your hopes up. The last six of these have turned up nothing."

It *coos*, full of reassurance in my head.

I wish I could actually understand what it says, but it speaks some language I don't know. It might not even be a language. It's nothing I've ever heard. Half of it doesn't even seem like I "hear" it now; some of what happens is a feeling, akin to emotion but not quite. The more I wear it the more I understand by feeling, but it's still a bunch of gibberish most of the time.

Sometimes it's like music in my head, sometimes like static between stations.

Bumping the car door closed with my hip, I stick my hands in its pockets and start walking toward the nightclub.

Sooner rather than later.

2

INSIDE THE CLUB doors is a swirl of colours and sound. Lights flash around from inside the main part of the club and the music rubs against me, muffled by the narrowness of the vestibule. The walls are covered in posters and flyers, stapled in haphazard layers of colours. They flutter at me from the back draft of my entrance like nervous doves pinned to the walls. Most of the pictures on them are men in cowboy hats, but there's a fair amount of women there too.

Hurrah for representation.

A man stands between me and the main area of the club. He's huge. I'm a little taller than average for a woman at five-seven and he's easily a foot taller than me.

And heavier than me by at least twice my weight.

Muscle lies on him like body armor, every cut and swell of his physique accentuated by a skintight black shirt that reads SECURITY across the chest. His skin is paper thin, traced with thick veins. He's jacked on steroids and maybe even some crank or meth or whatever is popular in this part of the country to cut fat. I can *feel* it radiating off him in a wash of chemically induced aggression. His jaw juts like a bulldog's and he has a foot-and-a-half-long flashlight in his hand, the kind bouncers love because you flash the intense light in a drunk person's face to disorient them and make it impossible for them to see when you swing the damned thing and it becomes a three-pound metal club loaded with heavy-duty D-cell batteries. It's a bonebreaker and a showstopper for anyone on the shit end of that particular stick.

No, I've never been on the receiving end of one.

Before all of . . . this . . . I was a peaceful person, and one who would never have gone to a club. Too many people, too many *men*, with too much alcohol flowing to be safe.

Too much like a Halloween party.

I move that thought into the vault in my head I keep for thoughts like that, pushing it aside before it takes root and blossoms into a weed of panic that will run rampant and make me have to leave.

I can't leave. I have things to do here.

Focus.

So I've never been to a club before.

But the dojo had a bouncer from a local strip club come in every few months and teach lessons on "dirty fighting." He was a surprisingly gentle man, barely taller than me, with fabulous muttonchops and soft brown eyes. He was fit but not intimidating until he clenched his fist and the roped muscle that ran from wrist to elbow would writhe under his skin like live pythons. He had a grip of iron and even Master Ken couldn't get free of it. (*In my line of work it's all forearm and steel-toed boots,* he told me once. *You lay hands on a disorderly customer you can't let them go or they will wreak havoc; you have to get them outside as quickly as possible.* I asked him how the boots helped. *You don't want to be slipping on some yahoo's spilled beer when you're dragging someone outside and a quick snap-kick to the shin with a steel toe makes anybody of any size more compliant like magic.*)

I glance down. The bouncer is wearing Reeboks.

He's still big though.

I take my hands out of the coat's pockets, shaking out the right one and flexing my fingers. The Mark, a sigil of weird geometry carved into my palm by an evil bastard chaos god, pulls from one side to the other, the scar tissue going tight.

I step up and the bouncer grunts, "Nice coat."

"Not particularly."

He stares at me, not quick enough to decide if I'm being a smartass or flirting with him. "Whatever," he mutters, and clicks on his flashlight, shining it at my chest instead of in my eyes. I haven't done anything to piss him off yet. He signals me to come closer. "ID and ten-dollar cover," he says.

I don't have my wallet. I left it behind weeks ago. I move closer, pushing a little bit of magick down into my hand. The Mark grows warm, heat sliding into the lines and swirls and squiggles cut in my palm.

His hand is out, him expecting my identification. I step close and he doesn't tense. He's not intimidated by me at all.

Good. Makes this easy.

I reach and brush my fingers over his. On contact magick crackles between us, rolling from my skin to his. I watch it trickle up the veins on his arm, making them glow from the inside out. He stiffens and his eyes go glassy, drifting slowly to my face.

I inhale to speak a spell and catch a whiff of him.

And the whole world slides sideways off the table.

3

My headspace goes white as my heart starts to hammer in my chest. All I can smell is the bouncer's body spray. *Tyler's* body spray. It fills my nose and I can't breathe.

Can't think.

My brain feels like it's jittering in my skull in time with the sudden, rabbit-fast beat of my heart and that thought I trapped a moment ago roars out of the vault, trying to claw-dig its way through my cerebral cortex, to burrow deep and complete.

Think. THINK.

I open and close my hands, flexing my fingers.

I can move.

I swing my arms, shaking them. From a distance I hear the sizzle of magick at the end of my right one.

I survived. This is not then. I am fine. Fine. Fine.

I feel the coat rustling around me. I am standing.

Tyler's dead. They're all dead. All the bastards who hurt me are d-e-a-d dead.

The thought splits the panic wide open, pulling me

back to myself. I come back with a gulp of oxygen in my lungs, dragging it in and pushing out the tinny taste of built-up carbon dioxide. My skin is clammy, damp, and it feels twitchy under my clothes, but I can see and, most important, I can think in a straight line again.

The bouncer hasn't moved.

Only a second, maybe three at the most, has gone by. Even if it felt like an eternity of panic, it was a blink of an eye. No time at all. Thankfully it's been so quick no one has come in behind me. I'm two steps back from the bouncer, but I can still smell him. Sax body spray. Boy's Nite Out scent. The choice of douchebags everywhere.

That's not true. I'm projecting. I can't help it.

I wish they would retire that damn scent. It's been around over ten years now. Trust me, I know.

The coat rustles around me, sensing my tension. I smooth my hands down it, trying to calm it, and realize that rustling is its way of caressing me, trying to calm *me* down.

I've got this, I think to it.

I do.

I take a deep breath, letting the taste of the body spray coat my tongue, all harshly bitter and chemical, and set my brain to analyzing it separate from the memory it's tied to, taking it as a flavor, an experience, dismantling the trigger it has become since that night. Working the problem like therapy taught me to. Mindfulness. Here and now. The panic pulses away, leaving me jittery as a rhesus monkey on a caffeine drip, but I'm good.

Functional.

The bouncer stands stone still, flashlight in his hand, eyes on me but unfocused, in the middle distance.

When I command him I raise my voice so I won't have to get close again. "My ID is fine and I gave you exact change for the cover."

He nods slowly. "Yes, Mistress."

Ah crap. *Mistress*. My magick has its hooks in him. He is now mine to call, mine to command. I could order him to give me all the money he's collected from the club and he'd do it. Order him to strip naked and dance an Irish jig in the cold outside.

Order him to kill himself.

Or someone else.

Shit.

It'll wear off.

I hope it'll wear off.

The door from the outside chimes behind me and in comes a gaggle of girls my age. They are loud, sloppy, and leaning on one another. They pre-partied in the parking lot.

They're my cue to move on.

"Have the best night at work you've ever had. Be nice to people, but enjoy it," I say to the bouncer.

"Yes, Mistress." His pit bull face breaks into a wide smile.

What? I feel bad for enthralling him.

One day I'll get used to my magick, but it's still a wild card sometimes.

When did that become a thing that I think? *My magick*. Just a few short weeks ago I was a regular girl . . . well, a girl anyways, and then my life got turned upside down by a chaos god I call the Man in Black.

Life since has gotten decidedly weird.

I leave the bouncer to the co-eds and walk into the main part of the club before I can think too hard about it and how screwed up it all is.

4

INSIDE SLAPS ME like an open hand.

Like I said, I don't go to clubs. I just don't. Never have. Not as a teenager and not in the last four years I could legally drink. I certainly wouldn't go to country-and-western bars even if I were so inclined. I don't hate country music. I went through my country phase like most people do, and I appreciate the concept of it, the drunken troubadour telling about life as most people live it. There is an honesty to be found in it, a rawness in the best of it that a lot of music lacks. People cry at love songs all the time because when pop music is sad it dresses up as happy to sell you the song. It's a used-car huckster selling you a lemon. Country music doesn't do that. It embraces the emotion of sadness. Sometimes it seems to promote it, seeking it out like a tongue worming against a broken tooth. A sad country song is a sad country song, but at least it's honest about that.

The song pulsing through the club isn't a sad one.

It's a modern, yee-haw, kiss-my-country-ass song. Fast beat, lots of twang, and drums that would be at home in a Nickelback tune. The middle of the room lies wide open and flat, a dance floor full of people in straight lines kicking their feet in time. The band onstage responsible for the music looks a lot more like rockers than rednecks; the singer is even wearing leather pants. A space with high-tops and tables is railed off to the left, and the right side of the club features a long bar lined with people.

I need to find the thing that brought me here, the thing I am hunting.

Reaching down inside myself, I push the energy that lives there, my magick, and feel it come, thrumming along my bones. The coat moves around me, whispering against my skin as the magick grows and wells. The circle of metal around my throat turns ice-cold as I center myself. It was given to me by a crack-whore love goddess in a condemned motel and acts as a focus for my magick.

"Show me," I softly say out loud.

Magick spins behind my eyes and my vision throbs and dials down until the room turns into a miasma of colours and feelings. I still see people, but now I see their base desires painted raw over them like auras. I see the desire in everyone, lime and chartreuse blending into saffron, the colours of loneliness and lust bleeding into each other. The colours taste like warm jasmine rice on my tongue, thick and aromatic, heavy on the back of my throat. Looking for love in all the wrong places. Saturday night slouching toward last call and nobody wants to go home alone.

At ten she's a two; at two she'll be a ten.

You don't gotta go home, but you can't stay here.

Hey, bartender, call me a cab.

Fine, you're a cab, now get the fuck out.

Here and there I find spots of cold blue, people who have given up and are simply drinking to numb the rest of their night until the harsh light of dawn cracks them across the face and they have to wake up in their skin for one more day.

Something snags my third eye.

In the far corner there's a clutch of hard darkness, an oil-slick black thorny bit of business. I turn my head to look at it directly, narrowing my eyes to see better across the darkened room as I study the person, looking through their desire-aura to find a young man. He can't be twenty-one, probably slipped the bouncer an extra twenty to let him in.

Focusing my attention draws his aura into my Sight. It slithers around him and, now that I'm paying attention, I can *hear* it like leather rubbing leather. The flavor in my mouth goes bad, tasting like worm dirt now, and I have to fight to not spit. Watching him is unsettling; my eyes want to move on. He sits at a high-top table with a bottle of water clutched in his hand. Dirty hair that's meant to be black hangs in shags and jags along the edges like he hacked it off himself; the bangs sweep low over eyes set in circles so dark that for a moment I think he's wearing a mask.

He keeps licking his lips.

He's watching people on the dance floor as they move, eyes wolf-tracking like they're sheep in a field. He looks to be focused on one couple in particular. The man tall and rangy, boxy shoulders and ropey arms in a plaid shirt that I can see the buttons shine on, legs poured into dark denim jeans with a crease starched sharp enough to cut paper. The man swings a girl in a circle of a dance, her big fluffy hair and big fluffy skirt swirling around a cute face and the thighs of a figure skater.

My brain automatically tries to decipher which one of them the kid is wolf-tracking when, from the other side, by the bar, a flare of magenta draws my attention.

At the end of the bar sits a girl about my age.

Did I ever *look that young?*

A mass of hair worn natural perches on her head. There are brassy chestnut strips of it that catch the neon lights inside the bar. Cowl neck sweater pulled low around her shoulders, she doesn't have much up top, but it's all on display. She's short and thick, nicely defined calves showing at the tops of slouchy boots, and she's smiling, smiling, smiling so big it makes hard lines at the corners of her eyes that I can see from across the room. She's gleaming in a haze of hot pink, her aura pulsing with excitement and desire.

But she's not the thing that caught my eye.

Standing next to her is something that looks human.

It leans on the bar, back to me, wearing a nice suit and a wide-brimmed hat. Long and lean and full of angles, it leans conspiratorially toward the girl, as if whispering all the secrets of the universe in her dainty ear.

It looks human.

The girl thinks it is human.

It has no colour.

It's a dead space in the kaleidoscope room, an empathic suck in a three-piece suit.

The girl stares at it as a long-fingered hand slips up to her face, gently taking hold of her jaw. In my magick-filmed eyes it looks like the hand of a mummy, desiccated and dry, sticks covered in cracked parchment. Under its elbow I watch its other hand moving over the girl's drink, the fingers rubbing together. Some sort of dust—*no, it's heavier than dust, separated into grains, sand*—sand falls into her drink.

Gotcha.

I shift my weight, heading toward them when the coat around me grows tight, pulling away.

Pulling toward the young man by the dance floor.

I look and what I see makes me draw in my breath.

5

A GUN.

A clunky, square semi-automatic that looks huge in his bony hand.

He's holding it low by his hip and he's still seated, but his whole body is tense, so tense he's vibrating. Cords stick out on his neck as he leans forward and the movement makes his bottom lip curl down and pull back in a snarl. His aura has blasted into a crackling blue and I can *feel* it against my skin even though I'm two dozen feet away.

I don't think, don't consider, I call my magick and make a wish.

And I blink out of existence.

It feels like a drop into a well, making my stomach lurch as if I've been shoved forward. A hard line of pain blossoms around my throat as the collar there constricts, but I'm ready for it. I'm ready for the drop. I'm ready for the wet rain feel against my skin. I've had practice.

And I have the coat. It protects me.

It's over in a nanosecond and I'm across the room, standing beside him. My hand clamps on his arm, the one holding the gun, and it makes his head jerk around toward me.

His mouth drops open and he's going to yell, to scream, to exclaim some shock, some fear, some amazement, something loud enough to draw attention, but before he can I tap my magick harder and make another wish.

It wraps tight around my chest and yanks me forward, dragging me into the raw red. My vision goes black and I flail out with my free hand toward where the kid is. My fingers find something soft, something fluttery like moth wings.

Hair.

I wrap my hand in it and close the fist, knuckles buried to his scalp, and pull him close. I hear him cry out, a harsh choke of sound against my shoulder, and I feel the coat stretch to cover us both before the wish completes.

We both blink out of existence.

6

THE TRIP IS longer this time. I wished us far away from the club, away from people.

Thankfully Arizona has a lot of open space.

We blink back into existence and I shove the kid away from me. He stumbles with a cry, jerking the gun up and around to point at me.

I don't move, holding myself upright even on shaky knees.

Wait for it.

The kid shakes his head, the gun rocking back and forth in his trembling hand. Greasy sweat coats his skin.

His eyes are glassy, slick surfaced like they've been coated in oil.

I know that look. I saw it the first time I wish-zapped Daniel.

"Lean forward, kid; otherwise you'll get it all over your—"

He lurches, hands flying to his mouth as his cheeks

puff out. The gun hits the sand about one second before the contents of his stomach do.

Interdimensional teleportation is murder on your stomach until you get used to it.

It's amazing what you can get used to.

While he pukes in the sand and grit I look around.

We're in the desert. I have no idea where in the desert we are but it is the desert nonetheless, all sand and rock and nothing much else. I didn't have time to wish specifically and I don't know shit about Arizona anyway. In hindsight, I guess I'm lucky my magick didn't send us to the moon. Now that I've had the thought, it does look a little like the surface of the moon, or maybe Mars, except the moon hangs high above us, looking large enough and close enough to tumble down and crush us. It's a big malevolent thing in the night sky, very nearly sinister as it paints the rolling dunes of silica in tones of lavender and blues. It's empty and desolate and I can't feel anything but the coat against my skin.

It's like I've been unplugged.

The magick in my bone and blood subsides from a screaming gale to a fragile murmur.

Other than the ragged breath of the kid at my feet as he pulls his shit together it is silent.

Silent.

In my ears.

In my head.

I take a deep breath and the air is clean in my lungs for the first time in a long time, so cold it feels like ice crystals spreading in my chest.

It feels bright. Pure. Untainted.

God, I could sit down in this peace forever.

The kid scrambles back from his sick, kicking sand with ratty shoes. His head jerks around, eyes white all around pupils so dark brown they look black in the moonlight. "Who . . . what . . . ?"

I watch him try to comprehend how we got to the desert. I didn't think before zapping us there; I just acted on instinct. In the bar, through his aura, he looked pure evil, but here, in the cold light of the moon, he just looks scared.

And jackrabbit small.

He isn't much taller than me and I might actually outweigh him, because he's all arms and legs. His pants are too big for him, belted across his hips instead of his waist, his shirt a long-sleeved thermal going ragged at collar and cuffs. Hard cheekbones plane down to a narrow chin, which makes his eyes look bigger than they are. His upper lip is dark, the beginnings of a mustache, but the rest of his face is preteen smooth.

He sticks that narrow chin out at me, trying to look hard even though he's still sitting on his ass. "Who the fuck are you?"

I don't take the bait. "Why are you trying to kill people?"

"Don't worry about it." He stands up. "How're we in the desert?"

"Don't worry about it."

He stares at me. I stare back.

I should leave him here.

He glares at me and I can see in his eyes the calculation of whether he is going to hit me or not. He wants to lash out, it vibrates off him, but something, probably being off-balance by the situation, is keeping him in check.

Or, maybe, he's just not prone to hitting women.

I'm going to leave him here.

I don't know where here is. It could be one mile out of town. It could be one hundred.

He was going to shoot people.

He doesn't look scary anymore. He looks scared.

He was going to shoot *people.*

I take another breath of that cold, clean air to clear my head and call up the magick inside me. The coat shifts around me in response and I blink, bringing my eyes back into magick sight mode.

The kid's aura has changed dramatically.

The blue is still there, crackling electric jags of fear, but now they zip through a nimbus of bright orange. The coat trills in my head, singsonging reassurance, liking what I see. I'm still not sure how much in my head the damn thing is, but that's what it feels like it's doing.

"What now?" the kid asks.

I shake myself into normal sight. "Hell if I know."

"You gonna leave me out here?"

"Actually, I'm trying to figure that out." The image of that girl and that thing flashes across my mind. I need to get back there.

He was going to kill people.

The Mark on my right palm grows warm.

His eyes shift past me, widening at something behind me.

I spin, the coat flaring around me.

Standing there is a dog with no skin.

There's distance between us, too much distance for him to close the gap in one leap, not enough to call us safe. His feet have sunk into the sand, grains of it stuck in long streaks up the legs. The moonlight paints his raw musculature the colour of uncooked liver, exposed knobs of bone and ribbons of tendon shining, reflecting the moonlight. The spine of him juts in a ridge of vertebrae that creaks slightly as he pants, rocking side to side in time to the whipcord tail swinging to and fro, to and fro, to and fro.

The sight of him makes me want to reach up, touch the top of my ear where the cartilage is frayed and torn, more gone than there. The skinhound chewed that off the first time we met. I keep my hand down, leave my hair over the ear, not going to give the damned thing the satisfaction of seeing the battle scar he gave me.

Why does this damned thing keep following me?

Since I left Daniel's side this skinhound has shown up time and time again. Getting a little closer and a little closer each time.

This is the closest he has come.

"That is one fucked-up-looking coyote."

The kid has moved up beside me. Close. Not close enough to

touch. The coat moves, the bottom of it slithering sideways to brush against his leg.

Hey, knock it off.

The skinhound tilts his skull, watching us through one lidless yellow eye set in a socket like a hard-boiled egg. The other socket is a black hole, empty and blind.

I did that the first time I met this thing, took his eye.

An eye for an ear.

The kid raises the gun he had. Sand sticks from where he puked on it. "You want me to shoot him?"

I raise my hand. "Put the gun down."

He doesn't listen, still pointing the gun at the skinhound. He holds the gun like he's in a video game, turned on its side, barrel pointed down at the end of an outstretched arm.

I remember the lessons I took long ago, Sensei O'leary clamping her wide hands on my arms, making me hold the gun upright and proper. Her husky voice echoes through the memory, honey-Irish accented and soothing. *If you hold your pistol like some kind of eejit, sideways like a rap video, you get a faceful of spent casings and you can't hit a damn thing. Don't. Be. An eejit.*

"Put down the damn gun."

"You crazy, *chica*. I'm gonna shoot that thing."

Watching the skinhound, I shake out my right hand, pushing magick down into the Mark there. It was warm already, but now it begins to glow red and crackle. I pivot and clamp down on the kid's arm near his wrist. I feel the backlash of the jolt I send; it's not much, but it's enough to make his hand convulse, dropping the gun.

Before he can say anything I open my mind, find what I'm looking for, and make another wish.

7

SPRING WARM RAIN sensation and a topsy-turvy jumble through what might be outer space and we blink into a dark, dank alleyway. The second our feet are solid on the trash-covered street I let go of the kid's wrist. The metal ring around my throat expands, loosening from skintight to lying on my collarbones as the wish-magick fades. My head swims just a second and I'm fever hot and my skin has gone all prickly under the coat. Three wish jumps in a short time and some other magick in between.

I'm pulling too much. Using too much reserve.

The coat shrinks, wrapping me tightly. Its weird, alien music/voice surges in my mind and I can feel it giving me a charge up. It's not healed all the way from where it rebelled and fought against its previous wearer, the Man in Black, the chaos god who started all of this. Maybe it would be if I stopped using magick and let it rest, but I keep pushing. I have to find that son of a bitch. For Daniel I do. For the last month the coat has lent me its strength, acting as a magick booster when I do too much.

I have magick inside me, but I've learned it can run out, get weak, get too low to use. I don't know if I could use so much of it I lose it, just burn out, burn up, and it be gone. When this all first started I would have welcomed that. Now the thought of losing it sends chills down my spine. But a girl's got to do what a girl's got to do, so I push it to the limits. When I do that it makes the magick look for other places to take energy from. For a while I used Daniel as a battery without knowing it. Now I use the coat. Yes, it is my magick. Yes, it is a part of me. No, I am not completely in control of it.

As soon as the wooziness passes I shake the coat loose from me.

The kid is sitting on a filthy milk crate that looks like it has been in this alley for a few weeks. He's trembling, muscles jumping under his clothes. My diabetic cousin does the same thing when his blood sugar plummets, mini convulsions. There's a small puddle next to him where he threw up again. I think it is anyway; it could be leakage from the Dumpster beside him.

Or someone else's sick that was already there.

The air reeks. Heavy, thick stink of rotting food and flyblowing even in the chill air. It lies inside my nostrils like a clot of rotting bacon and spoiled milk. I've worked in restaurants. Nothing stinks like those Dumpsters.

The kid shakes his head and rubs his arms. If he notices the stench he doesn't act like it. "Don't do that again. I'mma turn inside out you do."

His choice of words slaps me, triggering the memory of what I'd done to Tyler Woods.

He didn't mean it. He didn't. He doesn't know about that.

It still makes me snarl. "You don't know what it looks like to be turned inside out, punk."

Organs on the outside of bones, slick traceries of veins still plump with blood, lungs like soggy sponges lying over the glistening python coil of intestines.

It's one of the most horrible things I've ever seen.

One of the most horrible things I've ever done to another human.

Made more horrible by how I feel no guilt over it.

But the memory of how it looked like a pile of meat and offal, how it smelled like hot pennies, and how the moist warmth of it felt against the skin of my face still swims in the deep water of my dreams like a hungry shark trailing my bleeding psyche.

I've got to get away from this kid, get back on task. "Stay there," I growl, and begin looking for the thing I was hunting before.

The alley is long and straight, made from the back of the bar and a smooth cement retaining wall. It's cluttered, filled with junk besides the Dumpster, and a ratty van is backed across one end of it by a roll-up steel door and a ramp. The lighting is sparse, provided by the moon and intermittent square lamps mounted high on the back of the bar. It's a place of long shadows and inky pools of darkness.

A place for things to hide.

The band is still playing, their music coming through the wall of the bar like it's being smothered to death. It bounces between the sides of the alley, a slow-moving ghost, brushing against me with each step, dragging on my shins as I walk.

My eyes are jumpy, straining as I peer into every shadow. I can feel the thing from earlier here. I could use magick, but that would be like shining a spotlight on it. It would know I'm here, that I'm not just human and I'm hunting it. It might come after me. It will probably run. I don't want this thing getting away.

So I walk and I look.

And I hope it's not behind me.

The coat pulls at my arm, trying to make my hand rise, to reach inside, to go where it wants. I shrug it off.

Not yet.

Up ahead I see a pulsing line of light. Against the wall of the club, it's not bright, but it keeps going from so thin it almost disappears to a wide rectangular flash.

It takes me a second to realize it's from a door to the club that has been left cracked and is moving in the night breeze. There are four concrete steps going down from it. Deep shadows fill the area past it, on the other side of the light.

Moving shadows.

I quicken my pace, not caring if I'm heard.

Swinging wide, I come around until I can see inside the shadows. The thing in the suit and hat is hunched over the girl from earlier. Her head and shoulders loll to the side in a slump. She's perched on a pile of compressed cardboard, loose limbed and slack jawed. She's unconscious.

The thing straightens, its back to me. Its hands move, grab the girl's legs, and pry them apart.

Rage washes over me hot and sharp. I clench my right hand and the knuckles crack like small-caliber gunfire. It's heavy, swollen with magick that now roars through my veins, driven by a fuck-hot blind fury. The coat squeals inside my skull. Gobbets of raw red magick dribble off the Mark in my palm as I shove it deep into the pocket inside the coat. It's like sticking it in a bucket of arctic glacier water, sharp prickly burn of extreme cold. Frostbite under the skin. The Mark sizzles as my skin draws tight. My fingers find what they are looking for, scraping on silk cord braided over stone-hard teakwood.

I pull and it comes, sliding out of the pocket in one long sweep of blackened steel.

My hand is full of katana, black-bladed, razored death. Moonlight gleams along the narrow quicksilver line of the sharpened edge, tracing it from my hand to the tip and back again.

It's the sword of Nyarlathotep, the Crawling Chaos, the Man in Black. He lost the coat, he lost the sword inside it.

I drop my arm, holding *my* sword out and back, ready to strike, and I whistle.

It's a good whistle, one that cuts the darkness. The thing turns its head just enough to see me over its shoulder. Its eye is a pale smudge in the shadow cast by the brim of the hat.

"Hey, asshole," I say, "try that shit with me."

8

THE SWORD HUMS in my grip, my hand tight against the round *tsuba* that separates hilt from blade. The Mark on my palm *pulls* on the teakwood and braided cord like a magnet to steel. The magick in me connects to the sword, to the something inside it that makes it more than just a thing of sharp metal and wood. When I found the sword inside the weird pocket in the coat that has no sides and no bottom, just an endless biting cold, I studied it. Longer than the *shinai*, the bamboo sword I trained with in kendo, the blade has been formed of some black metal, so black it could be mistaken for onyx. The *tsuba* is of the same black metal and engraved with strange symbols around it that make my eyes hurt if I study them. The hilt sports braided silk over midnight dark teakwood. On a traditional katana, the braiding would be uniform, orderly, in a pattern that would not only ensure a good grip but also be an art form in and of itself. This sword, the braiding is haphazard, chaotic, forming no rhyme nor reason I can see.

And the sword is hungry.

No other word describes the feeling that radiates off the thing. It thirsts for blood, longs to bite through flesh, craves to cleave bone and sink into the marrow.

It whispers along my magick, drawing out that primal darkness we all carry in ourselves, coaxing out the murderous seduction of a stone placed in Cain's hand. It feeds the same dark desire that makes you want to jerk the wheel and hop the curb and mow down someone on the sidewalk just to see what they would feel like under your tires.

I hate using the damned thing.

I love using the damned thing.

Speaking of damned things, the creature lets go of the girl and turns toward me. Still unconscious, she slides sideways, spilling off the stack of cardboard and onto the ground. Her head hits hard enough for me to hear it *thunk* like a melon on the pavement.

Please let her be okay.

Maybe God will listen.

Maybe.

The thing straightens and I get my first full look at it in the dim light of the alley. My magick is thrumming in a loop through my body, from my Mark against the sword, to my heart, to my brain, and throughout the rest of me. My eyes are lit up with it and that burns away any glamor that might have fooled me inside.

The thing in front of me is bigger than a normal man, *far* bigger than me. Its shoulders hunch and its knees knock together, giving it a strange rocking shuffle as it comes toward me. Its face is round and pale, lips the same colour as its cheeks, but its nose is black, a flat oval stuck between big eyes and tiny mouth. It reminds me of something and I fumble around in my mind for what it is.

A teddy bear.

No, a koala. Koala bear.

The wide-brimmed hat isn't a hat at all but instead is the shape of its skull, the brim being a finlike flange that wraps its temples and flares like gills.

"You are one ugly bastard," I say.

It opens its mouth, making some garbled noise that sounds nothing like language, and stretches out its arms. Three multi-jointed fingers curl off each palm, tipped in a sharp bone spur meant to hook deep in muscle and hold. We are closing in on each other. I look down and I see that the suit it is wearing is torn open at the fly, the fabric ripped apart.

From the tear protrudes something completely alien.

It curls upward, the size of my forearm and covered with crystalline barbs that angle backward like porcupine quills. The hideous thing bobs at me as the sand dweller shuffles forward, thrusting its hips and moan growling.

Inhuman or not, its intention is obvious.

Pure rage flares inside me, smashing me flat and making me go ice-cold inside. I find that white static spot in my brain that shuts me down to fighting, to dealing damage.

No thinking. Only instinct.

Killer instinct.

I lunge forward, swinging the sword with every bit of strength I have.

9

SPARKS FLY AS the blade shudders to a stop against the creature's outstretched hands. I'm working the memory of my short training in sword use, leaning into the swing, using my whole body to drive the blade forward. This close I hear the grinding skritching scrape of metal on sand. The thing is crusted in it, like it crawled out of the desert we were in earlier. It dwells in the sand. My blow knocks some off and it flies into my face, crawling along the lower lid of my right eye. I blink, and the sight there goes blurry, washed in hot tears to cleanse the sand away. The collar of the coat flares around my jaw, fanning it away.

The sand dweller's mouth opens and its growls sound like a small creature being ground to death under a boulder as it shoves me away. I stumble, lashing out with the sword as I do. There's no aim, no intent other than to keep the blade between me and it. It leans away and then lunges behind my swing, coming in after me. I'm off-balance, way over my center of gravity, already falling from the shove. My body tenses, waiting for the impact. The coat flares around me, spreading like batwings along the ground. Tendrils sharpen to spikes, driving into the ground and anchoring me while the other side of it stretches, pushing me on around. It's like I'm in a harness on wires. I lean into it and turn with the spin as the creature misses and goes past me.

I whirl, coat whipping with me, sword at the ready.

The sand dweller doesn't keep running like I expect it to. Instead it leaps and hits the wall of the club, latching on with clawed hands and feet. Its spine bows, making a tall arch as more barbs rip from its skin in small sprays of sand. Its moon face breaks open and it pushes off, leaping and spinning in a long, slow arc, body twisting toward me.

Time contracts, pulling tight, and I see as if in slow motion, my eyes tracking the sand dweller's trajectory, pinned on my target. I hold until the thing hangs above me at the peak of its leap and move as it starts to fall toward me.

My blade flashes like quicksilver and I feel it bite deep and pull through. I strike blind, trusting my aim. Twisting with my momentum, I turn in time to see half the creature's penis strike the alley floor in a spill of sand like a shattered hourglass.

Take that, *you sick monster bastard.*

The creature lands wrong with a grunt that sounds almost mechanical, hitting the ground on its shoulder and neck and crumpling into itself.

The sword howls in my head, a long, plaintive cry, the sound a starving coyote would make if given only one morsel of food. It wants to drive forward, to hack the sand dweller into pieces.

I want to drive forward, to hack the sand dweller into pieces. The sword. It makes me want things.

The coat rustles around me, anxious.

My memory kicks and the first time I pulled the sword from the coat rushes into my mind.

10

PAIN SPIKED DEEP in my shoulder, the wavy horn digging, digging, digging, into the joint, driven by the straining night gaunt perched above me. I pushed with my other hand on slick rubbery skin, trying to send magick down to my Mark, but the pain was all there was. It swallowed me, chewed on me, rolling me into its grinding molars. The coat jabbered in my head, a gushing river of noise to the sunspot of agony that stole my vision, destroyed my ability to breathe, to think, to do anything. The horn hadn't stabbed through, held back by the screaming coat that covered me.

The night gaunt, silent, with no mouth to make sound, just a blank gray slate where a face should be, used its wide, draping batwings surrounding us to pull back. The blinding agony broke like the dawn. It leaned away, about to drive the horn back down, and I could see, for a split second I could see it rear back, slabs of oddly configured muscles bunching under slick rubber skin like a beluga, and I knew this time the coat would not save me. I would be gored, torn open by that twisting length of sharpened spur that *jutted from its skull. The coat flared along my chest lifting at the lapel as the sleeve contracted and pulled, yanking my arm across my torso and driving my hand into the gap it had made.*

My hand went ice-cold, plunged into the pocket, sinking farther than there was room for it to fit. The cold shocked me, running energy up my spine and into my brain. My vision went laser sharp, everything in hyper-focus. The night gaunt tilted its head, preparing to strike, when my fingers closed on the strangely corded handle of the sword.

The coat convulsed, dragging my arm out and the sword with it, blade up.

The night gaunt drove its blank face into the razored edge, splitting its own skull like a melon full of sticky black ichor that splashed across my face, drenching me.

My magick rolled through my Mark, connecting for the first time with the black-bladed sword of the Crawling Chaos.

Blinking my eyes clear, I pushed out from under the dead night gaunt and crawled to my feet. The sword shook in my grip as my hand clenched, locking down on the hilt, trying to meld my flesh with it. The sword roared in my skull, drowning out the coat, muffling my own magick, obliterating everything that wasn't its voice, its desire, its raw, greedy hunger. *My mouth went dry, throat closing as if I hadn't tasted water in weeks.*

The gore of the night gaunt soaked into the blade, drunk by the eldritch metal there. It wanted more. I wanted more. We wanted to spill all the blood of every living thing in all the world.

I plunged the blade into the dying night gaunt, right between those huge wings, eyes fluttering as the sword sucked up the swiftly fading life force of the monster.

Minutes felt like seconds, no, like thoughts *they were so quick, and the sword had drunk all it could from the dead thing.*

I pulled it free and looked around, seeking something else to slake the bloodthirst raging inside me.

I was alone, in an abandoned warehouse, in a burned-out part of some town somewhere.

But there was life nearby. The sword could sense it.

I could sense it.

I was halfway to the door before the coat was able to bind me and make me drop the damned sword.

I howled at it for hours until the influence subsided, slipping from my mind like water off glass.

And once it was gone I wept bitterly until the rising of the sun.

11

I LET GO and the sword hilt falls away into the pocket of the coat, its muffled wail trailing off in my head until it snaps off.

The sensation of that makes the skin crawl on the back of my neck and down my shoulders and I shudder.

"Damn, *chica*, that was some cool shit."

I turn to the voice and find the kid standing there. He's not shaking anymore and he's pulled his pants up some.

I glare at him, not sure what to say.

"How you make that sword disappear?" His eyebrows are pulled together.

"Magick."

He nods like he knows something. "I get that. My cousin, Jorge, he does that shit all the time, pulling coins from some *chica*'s ears and shit, hidin' cards up his sleeve. Always tryin' to get some, y'know what I mean?"

"It's not the same." His mouth moves and I jerk my finger at him, stopping him. "Don't call me *chica* again."

"What's your name then?"

Should I tell this kid my name?

Fuck it.

"Charlie."

"Javier." He smiles and it makes his eyes go sleepy looking. "You can call me Javi if you want." He pronounces it "hah-vee."

Out of the corner of my eye I see the sand dweller move, rocking like it is about to stand up. Putting my right hand into the outside pocket of the coat, I point with my left at the girl slumped onto the ground. "Go check on her. Take her inside if she's okay."

He glances at the girl and then back at me; the look on his face is unsure.

"I'm not asking, Javier."

"It's cool; it's cool." He moves off.

I watch him for a second, my right hand feeling around until it closes on what I'm looking for.

I walk over to the inhuman thing huddled on the alley floor.

I pull my hand out of the pocket.

In it is a knife as long as my forearm.

Idolcarver.

Blade of Castration.

The Knife of Abraham.

The Aqedah.

Holding it in my hand makes a tickle run from the back of my throat all the way to the deepest reaches of me. The handle is plain olive wood, worn shiny from generations upon generations of hands holding it. The blade is a triangle-shaped wedge of ancient iron with one sharp edge and a spine as thick as my finger. Holding it is the opposite of holding the sword. This knife was never truly the Man in Black's. It had been used to hack out idols to Moloch and then belonged to Abraham, who laid it against the throat of Isaac. Later, a Russian tsar and his castration cult used it to make the sacrifice of their own foreskin in some twisted ritual that went bad, really, really bad. The Man in Black claimed he took it from the bloody hand of a dying Nazi.

He's just fucked up enough for that to be true.

With it, I've killed the mad priest of a cancer god, an asshole who hurt me long ago, and stabbed the Man in Black to stop him from killing Daniel with it.

Now I'm going to use it to get some information.

Squatting next to the sand dweller, I grab the flange of skin surrounding its skull. It is hard under my fingertips and slick; the flex it has is stiff like thin plastic instead of pliable, like a fin instead of a flap. I give it a shake. The sand dweller snarls, but it's weak. There is a puddle of grainy mud spreading beneath it, bleeding out whatever it has in place of blood from the wound I dealt it.

Serves it right after what it was about to do to that girl.

I fight off the urge to go ahead and drive the Aqedah into its face and end it.

"Do you speak English?"

It growls something unintelligible.

Dammit.

I wish for us to understand each other.

The collar moves with the magick but not enough to hurt.

"Tell me how to find the Man in Black." My voice sounds weird in my own ears, distorted by the translation magick.

The sand dweller looks up sharply, eyes wide. I can see sticky grains of silica packed into the corners of them. "Who?"

"Nyarlathotep. Also known as the Crawling Chaos."

"He is not a man."

"Where is he?"

"You killed me. Let me die."

"Answer the question."

It moans and leans away. I flick the Aqedah out and slash the edge across its arm. The knife cuts deep, with all the resistance of warm cheese. The sand dweller howls again, jerking away.

"Next time I will cut off another whole piece of you. Tell me how to find Nyarlathotep."

"I know not where the Crawling Chaos has crawled to."

"You know something. Your kind always know something. Tell me."

It shakes its head.

I lift the knife.

"No, no, no, nonononono . . . ," it whimpers. "You found me; find him the same way."

"You don't think I've tried that, asshole? He's gone to ground and I need you to point to that ground."

"You've killed me. You have no threat."

I put the Aqedah in my left hand and open my right, lifting it in front of him. I pull up my magick and send it down my arm into the Mark there. Heat traces out the symbol, the intersecting lines, and the curling whorls that make it. The magick begins to ooze out of the Mark, painting him a hot magenta colour as thick gobbets of etheric energy drip off my hand, sizzling against the ground between us.

The words come from somewhere in the darkness inside me. I don't know them before I speak them but I mean them each and every one.

"Listen and hear and bear witness. I am the Hound in the Night, the Seeker, the Searcher, the Destroyer. I will chase your essence into the ether and I will harry it between my teeth. You cannot avoid me. You cannot escape me. You cannot outrun me. You are prey, mewling and broken in the outer dark. You will ask for the mercy of obliteration and find none at my hand. My plaything, my morsel, mine to keep, mine to kill, mine to destroy, and mine to harm."

With each syllable my magick grows, the excess of it spitting from my palm like the molten sparks from a welding torch. I feel it in my bones, slipping over my organs. It spills from my eyes and runs in hot tracks down my cheeks, shimmering free off my jaw.

Sheer, unmitigated terror lies on the sand dweller's koala face like a caul.

I lean in, mouth twisting into the savage, toothsome smile of a predator.

"Now tell me how to find the Man in Black."

12

———————

Dammit.

Dammit.

*God*dammit.

The sand dweller collapses in on itself as I stand and slip the Knife of Abraham into the coat's pocket. Sometimes otherworldly creatures do that when you send them off this plane of existence; their essence being the only thing that holds their physical form together, once you kick it gone the whole thing falls apart. One quick slash of the Aqedah across its throat and the thing was over for this world.

Maybe that's why killing them doesn't bother me. They aren't human. I've killed humans. Humans die; otherworldly things like the sand dweller are just released from their meatsuit.

Or sandsuit, in this case.

Sure, *that's* why it doesn't bother me.

What does trouble me is the thing it spoke before being released.

It said one name.

One damned name that confirmed what I didn't want to hear.

"Hey . . . Charlie . . ."

Javier is walking over. I look and the girl is gone.

"She okay?" I ask.

He looks confused for a second and then nods. "Oh yeah. She's good. Like she had too much to drink. But he didn't get to . . . well, you know. I sent her inside."

"Why didn't you walk her in?"

He lifts his hands. "No offense, but I wasn't doing that. Drunk white girl comes in from the alley with someone like me? Naw, ain't trying to get my ass handed to me."

I see his point. "I'll let it slide."

"Cool, cool," he says.

I turn away.

"Hey hey," he calls.

Javier is getting on my nerves. "What?" I say.

"What are you doing?"

"Leaving."

"Um . . ." His hands go deep in the pockets of his jeans.

"What, Javier?"

His mouth is pulled sideways. He's chewing the inside of his cheek. "Could I, like, go with you or somethin'?"

"No."

Hell no.

"Uh, okay."

I stand there, coat rustling around me. Javier doesn't leave.

"It's just . . . well, I never seen no shit like this. I want to see more." Slim fingers scrub along his scalp. "I can help."

"I don't do sidekicks."

"Not like that, *chic—Charlie.* I can help, like I just did."

"Go home, Javier."

His shoulders draw into a hard line, one that matches the angle of his narrow jaw. "I owe you. I was gonna do something stupid before I met you. You saved me."

Oh yeah, the gun. Fuck.

"I don't save people."

"Bullshit." Hands out of his pockets, he becomes animated, worked up, jerky motioned like a string puppet worked by an epileptic. "Bullshit. You saved Laura, you saved me, you—"

"Who the hell is Laura?"

The question stops him cold.

"The girl. Her name is Laura." He tilts his head like an owl, brows drawn tight over dark eyes. "You don't know her name?"

"I *wasn't* saving her. I was hunting the thing that attacked her. That's what you don't get, kid. If I had found that thing by itself in the desert I would have gone after it there. I wasn't here to save anybody. That girl, Lorna—"

"Laura," he interrupts quietly.

"Laura—whatever—" I continue, "and *you* weren't in the plan at all." The questions ride my tongue, pushing against the back of my teeth. *Why did you have a gun and who were you going to shoot?* But I clamp down and don't ask. Asking is just stalling, dragging my feet to avoid doing the thing I *have* to do that I do not *want* to do.

The sigh leaks out of me before I can stop it.

"Find help, Javier. Go into therapy, work it out, and get your shit together."

His face goes hard, bunching up like a piece of paper in a fist. I turn to go. His voice is thick, laden with accent as it reaches my ears.

"Hey, *chica,* your fucked-up *coyote* is back."

13

THIS TIME HE could close the space between us in one leap.

He could crouch on skinless haunches, raw muscles contracting with power, and be on me in the blink of an eye.

I go cold, adrenaline rush stealing my body heat, and slide into a fighting stance, moving my feet apart, lowering my center of gravity, spreading my arms. I don't have much left in the tank, but training takes over. The coat tightens around me, the tattered edges of it hardening into sharp spikes. It murmurs nervously in the back of my brain and I think:

I hear you.

The skinhound is panting, vivisected chest expanding and contracting, expanding and contracting, expanding and contracting. A long, raw-tuna red tongue lolls out between bone-cracking teeth, hanging off to one side as thick ropes of saliva swing in time to his breath.

We stand, staring at each other. Time laces tight around us.

I pull at my magick and it's sluggish, resistant. I've been pushing hard and I'm running low. I need to rest, recharge, replenish.

The coat murmurs louder.

I push its voice aside and my mind slides into threat assessment mode, working at high speed like I was trained to do in all the years of self-defense classes and martial arts.

The skinhound is close. I know how fast the damned thing can move and he's too close.

I don't have a weapon in my hand.

I don't have time to draw my weapon before the skinhound can reach me.

I'm diminished, low on strength.

I won't win.

Sensei Kim's voice rides over the singsong worry of the coat in my mind. *First option, run. Only fight if cannot run. Then* only *fight to be* able *to run. Run at first chance. Better to run and live than fight and die.*

I have enough strength for that.

I hope.

"Javier." I don't look back at him.

"Here." His voice is close and sounds tight. He's scared. I think. I don't know him well enough to really tell, but he sounds scared to me.

I don't blame him.

Moving easy and keeping my eyes on the skinhound, I reach back, hand outstretched. "Take my hand."

"Charlie . . ."

"Don't question; just do it."

I sense him move a second before his hand slides into mine.

His palm is sweaty.

I can only do this once (*can I do this once? do I have enough magick?*), so I pull the name the sand dweller gave me to the forefront of my mind.

The skinhound lifts his head, tongue rolling up into his mouth, and he takes a step closer. Razored crescent nails strike the asphalt. *Click-clack-click-clack.*

I clamp my fingers on Javier's hand as tight as I can, kick my sluggish magick in the ass, and wish with everything I have left.

14

Damn.

I can't see.

I can't hear anything.

I can't *feel* anything.

I'm locked in a cocoon of nothingness. I have been emptied out. I am without form and void.

Just after the realization that I have no feeling my brain kicks into gear, berating me in a voice that sounds a lot like my own.

You can't lie here—get up; get UP! Push through this!

I'm on my back. I can feel that now. Something hard underneath me.

Cold on the back of my head.

Move.

I open my eyes and the world floods in, but it makes no sense. Long stretches of metal loom above me, starting at the edge of my vision and rising straight up toward the clear night sky. Turning my head, I see tires, big tires about a foot from my face.

I sit up and I'm between two big-rig eighteen-wheelers in a parking lot. That explains the sloppy slick scent of diesel fuel and oil. I can hear the thrum of a highway nearby.

I need to stand up, need to find the kid, who's got to be close by, but I feel like hammered shit. Even the coat lies limp against my body, spent from five wish jumps in a short time. I've never teleported this much in one night.

Not since *that* night.

The night that started all of this shit.

The night the Man in Black walked into my life, made me an Acolyte, and dragged me into this world of magick, monsters, and bullshit.

Enough with the hate. I need to find Javier.

I roll to my knees and push to my feet. The coat tangles around my feet, almost throwing me back to the ground. It wasn't intentional—I hear the babble of its apology in my head, quiet murmuring along the bone in the back of my skull—it's just exhausted and slow moving like me.

As I stand, it hangs on me, feeling like a regular leather coat that is too big on me.

"Javier?" I don't shout it, just say it. He should be nearby.

I find him under the truck on my right.

He's curled up and shivering on the asphalt, but he's awake and it looks like he didn't throw up.

I hold my hand out. "Come on."

He shakes his head and it makes his whole body rock. "I can't do that thing again."

"Yeah, me either, but you're under a truck."

"I'mma stay here."

"Javier, you are under a truck. You can't stay here. Come out."

He glares at me. Somewhere nearby in the lot another big rig rolls by, close enough to vibrate the ground. I feel it through the soles of my shoes; I'm sure he feels it lying on the ground. He crawls out, ignoring my hand.

"What now?" he asks.

I point down the line of the trucks we're standing by to the warm yellow glow of the diner that sits in the middle of the lot. "Let's get something to eat."

I start walking and he follows.

"I'm not eating. That magick messed my stomach up."

I'm struggling to walk straight, my mouth tastes like I've been chewing mothballs, my head feels like someone has it in both their hands and is trying to twist it off my body, and the coat is dragging on my shoulders like it's made of wet cement, and *he's* complaining about a little post-teleportation upset tummy?

What a wuss.

15

———————

THE BELL OVER the door jangles as I walk in, gargling out a warning to all inside that we have arrived. The noise of it bounces around the inside of my head. I don't hold the door for Javier, but he catches it and follows me inside. Damn, it's bright, tubes of fluorescence slinging white light from the ceiling to bounce off the white tile floor and the matching white Formica counter that runs from one end of the place to the other. The only decorations in here are poster-sized prints of food evenly spaced along the walls, mostly breakfast, with a steak, a burger, and a bowl of spaghetti that looks like noodles coated in blood thrown in for variety.

Two waitresses perk up as we enter. They hawkeye us to see in whose section we'll sit. I'd bet it's been a slow night. Right now there are only three other customers, all scattered around the place in front of empty plates and cups, all looking like the same man from three different time periods.

One is young, has a beard and longer hair under a cap. He's hunched over a phone his fingers are flying over.

One is middle-aged, thicker than the first but still similar, cresting the hill of life and sporting a shorter beard and hair than the first with gray touches but also wearing a cap. He's hunched over a newspaper.

The third is old, grandpa old. Gray and bent and twisted like a piece of driftwood. His cap is battered and filthy and his beard is nearly pure silver save for the yellow patina of nicotine around his mouth. He hard-knuckles a steaming mug, his eyes the same milky colour as his coffee when he looks up at me.

My life is so weird I actually stop and think, *IS this the same man from three different timestreams?*

Probably not.

And if so, it doesn't have anything to do with me.

Probably.

I move to a booth on the far end of the diner and put my back against the wall just in case.

The old man lifts his cup as I slide into the booth and gives me a nod before dropping his eyes.

And now I want coffee more than I ever have before.

Javier slides in the other side of the booth. His fingers slip over the hard plastic tabletop. The menu is printed underneath it. Dozens of items with pictures laid out before us, divided straight down the middle so he has his menu and I have mine.

"Damn, they got a lot of food."

"You hungry now?"

"Might be so. My stomach feels better, not like it's flopping around inside me anymore."

"Got any money?"

His eyes flick up at me and his cheeks get darker. I pretend to not notice. "Yeah, I got some."

"Some I can work with. Order what you want then."

The shorter waitress has broken off and is moving toward us, coffeepot in hand. She arrives and puts two mugs down. I nod and she fills mine.

Javier pushes his away. "I'll have a cola."

"I'll bring it right over." She smiles big and it feels fake, strained, but hey, that's her job. "You need anything, dearie?" she asks me.

Dearie? What the hell?

"Creamer."

She nods. "Ready to order? Everything on the menu's available twenty-four hours a day."

I order the red-eye special: country ham, mixed greens, and sweet potatoes. Javier goes with a bacon cheeseburger and fries. I drink the coffee and it begins working its way into my system, sharpening me like steel on stone. Javier's fingers never stop moving, touching everything in a round-robin of fidgeting.

"Knock it off."

He freezes and looks down at his fingers on the salt and pepper shakers. He pulls his hands in and drops them to his lap out of my sight.

"What happened to your ear?"

It's not the question I expect and my hand is halfway there before I catch myself and stop it. I shake my head though, not that my hair is long enough to cover the top of my left ear, the one he's asking about, the one with four jagged rips in what's left of the cartilage on the top rim. The one that looks like a piece of mangled plastic.

"Got bit by the skinhound."

"The fucked-up coyote?" He says coyote as "ko-yo-tay" in one long, warbling almost syllable.

"Yeah." I look at his face in the bright light. This close I can see the dark line of the split on the corner of his lip. His left ear hugs the side of his head, but the right one pushes out, looking like a wad of chewed bubble gum. Cauliflower. "What happened to yours?"

The skin under his eyes goes dark, flushed with blood, and he looks away. "Wrestling. At school."

I study him, looking over his narrow shoulders, long, thin arms, and lack of definition to his trapezoid muscles. There were grapplers at the dojo I studied at back home, mostly jujitsu fighters but some Greco-Roman wrestlers, and they were built wide on the top. Hours and hours of practice, the amount of hours it would take for him to build enough scar tissue in his ear to cauliflower it, changed their bodies. It spread their chests with lats, the slabs of muscle that makes wrestlers look like cobras when they flex and thickened their necks and shoulders into steel cables. I compare his slight figure to theirs.

Javier isn't a wrestler.

He's lying.

I let it go. It's not like I don't understand lying to new people.

"So, where are we?"

I nudge toward the logo across the top of the menus and read it out loud. "'Mabel's. Home of the best food east of the Mississippi.'"

"East?"

"Probably."

He thinks for a long minute. "I guess that's why the air smells different here. Don't smell like concrete."

I just take a sip of coffee. I didn't notice a difference in the smell of the air. The waitress comes over with our food and slides it in front of us with a practiced lean.

"Excuse me, ma'am," Javier says, and his manners surprise me. "What state are we in?"

"You don't know what state you're in?" She breaks into a big grin. "Why, I'd say a state of confusion then."

"We've been driving all night and must have missed the sign."

"Shoot, darlin', you two have made it to the great state of Kentucky."

Javier smiles and it's warm and it makes his face turn into . . .

something. Not handsome but attractive. If you like that sort of thing. He winks at me. "Told you, Sis."

"Yeah, you were dead on the money," I say.

The waitress laughs and touches him on the shoulder before walking away with a promise to check on us real soon. I guess she likes Javier's smile.

Once she is gone I raise my eyebrow at him. "Sis?"

He smiles again, smaller this time. "I didn't want her to think we were a couple and, y'know, ruin my chances."

"First of all, slick, she's all grown-up. You're way too young for her."

"I'm almost eighteen and she ain't too old." He glances around at her. "She could take me under her wing."

"You're going to move to Kentucky, settle down, start making babies, and what? Work here at the truck stop?"

"Chill, chill; I'm just goofin'."

"You're not funny," I tell him.

"Maybe, but it was slick how I came up with that cover story, right?"

I shrug.

He takes it as a yes. "Yeah. Told you I could help."

"You're right; you absolutely saved me from the waitress discovering I don't have a car."

"You didn't know what state we are in."

I shrug and take a bite of ham. It's a little tough and has a few streaks of dark brown caramelization from the griddle, but the flavor of it lights up the inside of my mouth with saltiness. City ham is sweet, the kind of ham you have at Christmas; country ham is mostly for breakfast and is cured like they used to cure ham, with a thick layer of salt and a ton of smoke. The sodium is off the charts and I feel it raising my blood pressure almost immediately. It's so good I talk with my mouth full. "*I* can leave here as easy as I came."

He starts eating and we don't talk for the next several minutes. I guess his stomach is better because he makes short work of the burger. So I lean into my meal and at the end of it I feel full and my plate is clean.

I also feel better.

Not completely recharged. I still need some sleep, but I'm not going to collapse anymore and I can think.

Javier has leaned back and slouched down on his side of the booth. His eyes are half closed and his thin fingers intertwine across his stomach. "What now?"

Before I can answer him the bell over the door jangles out a warning and in through the door walks an ancient being of incalculable power who sees me, smiles crookedly, and heads in my direction.

16

ASHTORETH.

The Scarlet Harlot, Unholy Ishtar, Concubine of Chaos, and Whore Goddess Galore.

Glory hoary hallelujah.

She stands in the harsh white fluorescence looking better than she did the last time I met her lying in a puddle of other people's fluids on a filthy mattress in a run-down slum of a motel. She doesn't look like a crack whore this time, doesn't really look anything like she did last time, but I still know her. Now she looks *young,* far younger than before, falling into the raw bloom of early womanhood. Crow-haired and sullen-eyed, she's long and lanky under a bright yellow slicker too short to cover more than her torso, leaving coltish legs sleek and bare to stretch from its bottom hem to the floor. The clothes under her raincoat are inconsequential, some kind of ragged little skirt and a scrap of cloth that covers a nearly-flat-but-in-no-way-boyish chest. The sunshine colour of her slicker glows in the harsh light, giving a buttery haze that makes her complexion look even darker.

She looks nothing like she did before, but I know it's her by the feel of her in my blood and the electric buzz in the torc around my throat.

She begins walking toward our booth.

I slide out and stand. "Javier, get over here."

The kid doesn't question. He jerks up and moves fast, coming around the table and into my side of the booth like a jackrabbit.

From the corner of my eye I see him look up at the approaching goddess of desire and surreptitiously slide the steak knife I used on my ham somewhere out of sight under the table.

He's not dumb.

The closer Ashtoreth comes the more her hips sway, moving from side to side like a pendulum, the stiff latex of her raincoat swinging like a bell. Each bump and grind of her narrow hips makes her skirt ride up, sliding higher and higher and higher until I know she isn't wearing underwear. A few feet away she lifts her arms, stretching them out as if to hug me.

I put my hand out flat.

She draws short and frowns.

I indicate the empty side of the booth and she slides in surprisingly ladylike, straightening her skirt and moving primly.

I sit across from her, beside Javier.

She smiles widely and her teeth are intact. The first time I met her, the last time I'd seen her, there was a circle of missing teeth that had been eaten away by the corrosive smoke from a crack pipe. Now her teeth are all there and covered by the remains of a set of old-school braces, rectangles of dull gray steel cemented to the enamel and tiny bits of broken wire rimmed in watery pink from where they've cut the insides of her lips till they bleed, just a little, all the time. If it hurts, she doesn't seem to notice.

Maybe that's why her lips look so full, nearly swollen.

Her eyes are glassy, the pupils dialed down to pinpricks, and they jitter in their sockets. She's looking at me, not around, but even staring straight ahead her eyes shake side to side as if some tiny creature inside her head is chewing on the optic nerve in the back of her eye socket. Her skin is smooth but waxy looking, shiny from not being washed.

She smells slightly sour.

Like milk left to sit out all night.

"Hello, child." Her voice is raspy, like her throat is sore from a cold coming on or she had strained it.

"Ashtoreth."

"Did you come to take me up on my offer?"

I almost ask her what she means and then her fingers tug slightly at the cuff of the slicker and it hits me, the image of her the last time I'd laid eyes on her.

Still, I owe you my gratitude." The Whore Goddess rose, kneeling on the soiled mattress. She stretched out her arms and the wound gaped open, starless void yawning wide. "Would you like to fuck my wound?"

Ashtoreth's terrible giggle chased me down the hallway.

I repress a shudder.

"That will never happen," I say.

She frowns. "*Never* is such an ugly word."

"*Never.*" I put more force behind it.

She shrugs and her face pivots toward Javier. She licks her lips.

"Don't." The word comes out in a snarl and she looks at me like I've spit on her instead of just speaking.

"My, my, I didn't take you to be the polyamorous type, Acolyte of Nyarlathotep."

"That's not my name or my title."

She tilts her head and stares at me, thick eyebrows creasing. The movement makes the slicker squeak against the vinyl of the booth seat. "No. I guess it is not."

"Never mind that; just leave him—"

"What do I call you?" she interrupts.

I catch the phrasing. "You don't need to call me."

Those dark eyes light up and focus on me. "Ah, you have learned a thing or two since we last saw each other."

I shrug.

"How do I address you then?"

I sigh. The Man in Black used to call me by either my full name of Charlotte Tristan Moore or a title. Ancient beings take names very seriously. "*Charlie* is fine."

"*Charlie* is what your friends call you." She smiles and it is full of dark promise. "I did not know we were so . . . *intimate*."

"We aren't intimate."

"If you speak it then it must be true . . . *Charlie*."

I want to slap the smug smile off her face.

Javier leans forward. "I'm Javier, but you can call me Javi."

Ashtoreth giggles. "Javi! Such a sexy name for a sexy young man."

"That's right, *mamacita*."

"Javier, stop," I say.

Ashtoreth acts like I said nothing. Her voice undulates across the table, writhing around the words she is using. "So sexy. I bet you could do things to me that would make me scream. Are you sexy enough to make me lose my mind, to make me scream your name to the wild wastes for the dire wolves to hear?"

Javier jolts beside me, practically climbing over the table.

Ashtoreth licks her lips, her voice a whiskey-dark growl. "Come show me."

Javier pulls his legs up into the seat and lunges as Ashtoreth giggles. I throw my arm out, pushing him down, and he turns to me, eyes wild and full of rage. I see it crawl up into his expression. Another second and he will hit me to get away.

Then I remember the knife he took from the table.

I shove my elbow into him and lean, pressing him into the corner of the booth while putting my Marked hand against my mouth. The raised lines of scar tissue on my Mark rub all slick-hard over my lips and I lick them. The body fluid crackles across it, igniting a connection to the magick inside me. It's still low ebb, only a little replenished from the food, but I don't need much.

Javier has started to jerk against me as I slap my wet palm against his arm, spark my Sight into effect, and strip away the world that we know.

17

My vision flashes like a power surge, flaring bright and then dulling into a weird amber glow. I can still see the booth and the diner, but everything else has changed. I can feel Javier at the end of my magick and I know he's seeing the same thing I am.

Ashtoreth is still across the booth from us, but now her body fills the other side. Her breasts lie on the table in loose skinsacks that jiggle across their surface like the skim of milk gone warm. Her skin is mottled, dark spots gathered across her arms, chest, and face like moss. The rest of her is tinged a shade of suffocation blue and has the wrinkly look of plastic over cheese. Her face is now a hatchet wound, split into a raw fissure from brow to chin with round yellow marbles for eyes that protrude on each side of it. They shine and their light makes deep shadows on the edges of the wound that is her face. Her hair slithers around her shoulders as if alive.

"*Madre Dios!*" I hear Javier say. My hand jerks and he pulls out of my grip.

I can blink and break the Sight, but I hold on for a moment.

There are lines of energy running from the three men to Ashtoreth. They zig and zag through the diner, bubbling streamers of liquid energy that flows into her.

Interesting.

I exhale sharply and break the magick, letting it fall inside me to lie on the floor and shake like an exhausted animal.

18

JAVIER SHAKES BESIDE me.

A leaden weariness has crept back into my bones, but I sit straight and pick up my coffee to hide it. The coffee has gone cold and the creamer is starting to separate from it, but I swallow and act as if it is the most delicious thing I have ever tasted.

Ashtoreth still sits across the booth, looking human again and frowning.

"What was that?" Javier asks.

"*That* is what she really looks like."

Ashtoreth frowns. "You revealed me to him?"

"Yeah."

"That is . . . uncool."

I just shrug and let slide the strangeness of slang coming from her mouth.

He stares at her for a long moment, then mutters, "Madre Dios."

"Remember that the next time she tries to seduce you."

"I can't believe it."

"Believe it."

"But how . . . ?"

Ashtoreth twirls a lock of hair. From somewhere she has a piece of well-chewed gum she uses to blow a big pink bubble that stretches thin enough to see through before tearing apart and collapsing to be drawn back inside her mouth. "You'll never understand how, Javi," she says. "Magick and physics are incongruously compatible."

"But you're so—"

She cuts him off with a sleepy snarl. "I don't owe you pretty, *human boy.*"

"Let's stop with the games," I say.

"Existence is a game, Charlie. You should learn that."

"I need your help."

She laughs and it shakes her shoulders up and down. She keeps laughing, leaning forward as strands of black hair fall loose around her face. When she sits back there are tracks of glycerin tears on her cheeks.

"I don't know why you found that so funny," I say.

"Humans asking gods for help, that is humor at its finest."

"You helped me before."

Her teeth show. "Not you, *him,* and under *threat.*" She tilts her head sideways, looking at me. "Did you forget that part?"

"I didn't forget." I still remember how the Man in Black treated her, with dismissive, casual abuse.

"What can you threaten me with?"

The look on her face.

Her jittery eyes are drowning me. She's not looking at me with defiance or anger, but a profound sadness that radiates off her, a sense of desperate *need* mixed with something I can't put my finger on, but it cuts me, slicing to my bone marrow.

Shame.

It's shame that it is mixed with.

And, all of a sudden, I'm tired again. Not just in my body, but in my soul. I search for the words to tell her how much I don't want to hurt her. I don't want to hurt anyone.

Except the Man in Black.

I don't even want to hurt him, I just want to kill him.

"Inside this coat I wear, a coat that lives and holds power on its own, I have the cursed blade of the Crawling Chaos. I have the Aqedah, holy knife of Abraham, at my right hand. I own the soul gem of an elder god. Around my throat I wear the torc you gave me of your own power." I raise my right hand, fingers spread to display my Mark. "And most of all, I bear a magick inside me that I have used to kill and destroy and drive away things like you that would cause harm to humanity."

One by one, I fold my fingers down into my palm, covering my Mark.

"Sitting here tonight, I offer none of these things as a threat."

Her mouth has gone slack, bottom lip out, as she stares at me.

I reach out my hand, opening it palm up. "Instead, I offer them to you in friendship and protection. I will use them, with your help, to track down the one who threatened you, to find the Man in Black, and to make him pay for the insult offered to both of us."

Beside me Javier crosses himself.

Ashtoreth's eyes flick from my face, to my outstretched palm, and back.

"You would be my friend?"

"I would try, Ashtoreth. I truly would."

She nods.

"I accept." Her hand slides into mine and it is warm like a human one would be. "Charlie."

19

———

THE DARKNESS IS warm and it wraps me close.

I snuggle down into it and I don't want to climb out. The world around me rocks gently and everything is soft.

Wait.

Where am I?

I jerk up and open my eyes. It's dark, but I can see. It's a closed space, walls and a roof close above. I'm sitting on something wide and flat and brighter than the walls and ceiling. It's soft. A mattress. I'm on a mattress. To my ears comes a softly grinding *whub–whub–whub* noise that fills the space around me.

I'm on a mattress.

A mattress in a truck.

A truck moving down the road.

In just a second all of it clicks into place, burning away the sleep-fog in my brain, and I remember Ashtoreth helping me and Javier into the back of a box truck half full of new mattresses.

Javier.

I turn and find him lying next to me but lower, the curve of his spine pressed against my thigh and hip.

The bottom of the coat around me is spread over him like a blanket.

I whisper, "You jumping ship for the new guy?"

My head fills with its musical babble. It's urgent and reassuring and sounds stronger than it did back at the truck stop. The coat shifts, beginning to pull away from Javier, coalescing back toward me. I put my hand on it. "Stop. I was just kidding."

The coat relaxes back in place over his thin form, but it's too late; the movement has woken him. He stretches and yawns.

In the dark I can see when he opens his eyes.

And when he smiles.

"Hey, Charlie."

He is still pressed against my leg, through the coat, but against me. His voice is throaty and familiar.

Too familiar.

Nope.

I scoot away to the edge of the mattress, bracing my back against the side of the truck, turning to put my feet and legs, the strongest striking limbs I have, between me and him. I can feel the vibration of the road under the truck tires more acutely through my back.

The coat drags off him, going with me.

He rolls over on his side and watches me, still lying down.

What is wrong with this situation?

Javier is acting like we've known each other for years instead of hours. Comfortable. Familiar. Friendly.

Not freaked out to be hundreds of miles from home with a stranger who wish-napped him into a world of monsters and whore goddesses.

And why am I so calm?

I'm in the dark. In a closed-in space. On a mattress. With a strange man.

I should be in total freak-out mode right now. My *shit* should be *lost*.

But it's not. I'm not.

My mind is clear and I'm objective.

I hold no panic.

No fear.

Is it Javier? Never before has it mattered. Any man being that close would have triggered a body memory.

Except with Daniel.

The memory of the night we had both professed our love for each other and kissed before falling into my bed fully clothed and exhausted sweeps through me. With Daniel I'd had no panic. I trust Daniel. I love Daniel.

And he loves me. I know it and not just because he said the words.

I don't love Javier. I don't know him enough to even trust him, although I do feel weirdly protective of him.

Maybe that's it? Maybe. Doesn't feel right. Keep looking.

Is it some mojo Ashtoreth performed?

I don't feel spellcast. No fuzzy head, no thoughts that are sharp edged and foreign in my brain. No weird wire burrowing into the folds and creases of my personality trying to stitch over my innate distrust and hard-won paranoia. My skin isn't tingling. I don't have a nose full of any arcane smells.

I don't think it's that.

Javier sits up, crossing his legs. I can see him swaying with the rhythm of the rocking truck movement. "What's wrong, Charlie?" he asks.

I answer him honestly. "Nothing."

"Why are you being weird then?"

"Because nothing is wrong. Absolutely nothing is wrong right now."

"And that's a bad thing because . . ."

"Because things *should* be wrong right now."

"Okay."

I take a deep breath, moving words around in my brain to explain. You know what? I don't feel like explaining the whole thing.

"Just trust me, Javier. I should be freaking out."

"But you aren't."

"I am not."

He shrugs. "Seems okay to me then. I wouldn't question it."

"Listen to me. In my world, this world you're tagging along in, you have to question everything. You cannot trust anything to be just what it appears to be. You don't question you can wind up dead or worse."

"Worse than dead? Now you're just being dramatic."

"You've already forgotten what you saw back at the diner?"

He shudders. "Oh hell no. I won't *ever* forget that."

"That's what I mean. That right there."

He nods. "Okay. I'll follow your lead."

"Don't follow my lead. I'm making this up as I go along. Keep your wits about you."

"You'll keep me safe. You're badass, Charlie. I know you will."

Oh, Javier.

"Where's Ashtoreth?"

"The *mamacita* from the restaurant? She said she was riding up front."

"I hope she didn't ditch us."

His frown is a dim shape on his face in the low light. "Didn't you find her this last time?"

I nod. I don't know if he can see it between the dark wood of the truck wall, my dark hair, and the upturned collar on the coat, so I speak out loud. "Well, I didn't zap us to that diner for the food."

"My burger was pretty tasty. They grill it up good in Kentucky." He says *Kentucky* like he says *coyote*, low and run together with an emphasis on the middle syllable: "ken-tooooo-kee." "You didn't like yours?"

"My food was fine." I remember that ham. "Better than fine, it was really good."

"But we went there for . . . what was her name again?"

"Ashtoreth."

He mutters it a few times before nodding his head. I guess he has it now.

I don't know how long this ride will be, where we could be going, why we are in a mattress truck, but it looks like Javier is with me.

Might as well get into this while it's just the two of us.

"What's up with you?"

"What do you mean?"

"Back at the club."

He is slowly turning away from me. "What about it?"

"Jesus, Javier!" I snap. "You had a fucking gun and were going to open fire in that place. What did those people do to you?"

"Those people? Wait, do you think I was going to light up the whole place?"

"What else could you have been doing?"

His head drops, chin to chest, his silhouette becoming strange. It takes a long minute of just listening to the road rumbling under the truck for him to speak. "I wasn't going to shoot everybody."

Something in his voice tips me off. "Who were you going to shoot?"

He mutters something. It doesn't sound like English, not alien/weird/supernatural, just not English. Maybe Spanish. The pain radiates off him. The coat trills in my head and the edges of the hem flutter across the mattress between us, softly caressing Javier's leg.

I let him go silent for another few minutes.

"Javier."

"Yeah."

"You can tell me."

"I was going to bust a cap in Fonso."

"I don't know who that is."

"My mom's *esposa*."

"What did he do?"

The energy off Javier jolts, running up through the coat and into me. It's jagged and hard and brittle like a fist made of splintered glass. "What *didn't* he do?"

I hear the tears even though I can't see them.

"It's okay, Javier. Let it out."

He groan/screams, a low, guttural noise that tears from deep inside him. I know that sound. I've *made* that sound. That sound hurts coming out.

"He came home with my mom when I was little, maybe five, six, something like that. He never left; he was just there one morning when I got up."

"When did he first hit you?"

"What?"

"When was the first time?"

"How did . . . never mind." He shudders. "It's hard to remember. Might've been that first day. I was young."

"Did he do that to your ear?"

The black shape of his arm in the dim light shoots up to the side of his head. "He's left-handed."

So he hits on the right side.

"Does he hit your mom?"

"Yeah."

Fuck, this kid is fucked up. I've had a lot of therapy in my time, since that night. I know fucked up when I see it. He needs help, a therapist or counselor.

(Or a gun?)

Shut up.

Too bad therapists are in short supply in the back of a mattress truck going down the road.

Fuck.

"That make you run or stick around and try to keep him from hurting her?"

"I can't stop him. You saw him; he's huge, all built, and tough.

I tried stopping him and when I did he knocked me unconscious and put my mom in the hospital for two days."

I study him as much as I can, pulling the picture of Fonso in my mind, accessing it. I picture the man in the bar Javier was wolf-tracking. Taller than Javier and heavier, but I wouldn't call him huge. Then again, none of Tyler Woods's crew were all that big, but in my mind for years they were all-powerful monsters. I can see where Javier has a skewed perception. "He's been doing this shit for what? Ten, twelve years?" I don't need Javier's nod to know I'm right. "Does he do anything else?"

"What do you think?" he growls.

"Oh, Javi . . ."

"Don't you dare be sorry for me, chica! Don't fucking dare!"

Something wet hits my cheek. It's not big, probably spit, he's upset and crying, and I'm sure it's not intentional.

"I don't know what it's like, but I know something of what it is like."

"You don't know shit."

I put the heat into my voice as I echo the words of my favorite therapist. "Don't let your pain make you an asshole."

It makes him visibly start.

"You're right. I'm sorry."

"Don't be sorry; just don't think you have a lock on pain. There's too much of it going around for that."

"Did your father?"

"No!" It's too loud, too fast, the words moving out of my mouth like bullets. My dad has been nothing but there for me through what happened and the idea . . . it just makes me react like I do. "God no. But people have hurt me, Javier. I know what that is."

"What did you do about it?"

Turned my first rapist literally inside out with magick by accident, making him a steaming pile of meat and bone and blood.

Watched the second one be shot by the third because I severed his forearm with the Aqedah and then watched that one bleed out.

Watched the last one get cut in two by the Man in Black, using the sword that is inside my coat.

"I had a shit ton of therapy."

Javier snorts dismissively. "Therapy? Must be nice to be a white girl."

"The fuck does that mean?"

"Means I can't afford no therapy."

"You can afford a gun?"

"Guns are easy where I'm from."

"After all those years of taking it, why not just leave?"

"Couldn't."

"Why . . ." I stop talking. I know why. "Brother or sister?"

"Sister. Aricelia."

"How old?"

"Almost ten."

I don't say anything. It will come.

"I caught him watching her sleeping."

"You think he would . . ."

"He told me he would when he was doing it to me. As soon as she 'got her growth.'"

Oh.

Fuck.

That sits between us, a dark, ugly thing.

He slides closer. "That's why I need to go with you. I'll help you. You make Fonso disappear."

"I can't do that."

"Bullshit."

Could I do that? Kill a human?

A human *not* tied to this elder-god-otherworldly shitstorm?

Probably.

For this? Yes.

"Javier . . ."

He moves close enough for me to see the tears on his cheeks. "Please, Charlie, don't make me beg."

Gravity shifts, pulling at me. Javier leans with it. The truck is slowing down. It rocks sharply left, then right, and drags to a stop.

Javier slides back. "I think we've arrived."

I slide to the end of the mattress and drop to the wood floor of the truck.

I don't look back at him; I just say the words. "First chance we get, we go take care of Fonso."

He slides down beside me. "I knew you were a hero, Charlie."

Oh, Javier, please don't rush to judgment on that.

20

———

WE'RE BOTH STANDING when the back of the truck rolls up on a track. Light and heat run into the opening, turning the cool dark into a stifling box around us in seconds. Ashtoreth smiles up at us, standing next to the grandpa from the diner. He reaches up an arthritic, swollen-knuckled hand to help me down. I step off the back of the truck and drop. The coat flares around me and I bend my knees to absorb the impact, but it still shocks me across both shins like someone hit them with a Louisville Slugger.

Sometimes I'm stubborn.

Javier swings down using a strap bolted to the outside of the truck like that was its purpose for being there. The movement is graceful, almost catlike.

Grandpa shrugs and grabs the long chain attached to the rolling door and yanks on it. The door falls quickly, slamming into place. He throws a lever and locks it down.

I glance around.

Wide parking lot full of cars and trucks. Second parking lot with longer spaces outlined in white paint that holds semis and RVs. One short brick building with a bathroom on each end and five, no, six soda and snack machines between them. Picnic tables and trash cans in the grass to one side. A bank of pay phones. (Pay phones? Are those even a thing anymore?) I can see the highway on the other side of the building and hear the *thrum* and *whoosh* as vehicles fly by.

A rest stop.

We are standing in a rest stop on the side of a highway in Kentucky.

Maybe Kentucky. It's daytime, feels like afternoon, and bright. We could be in another state by now.

I start to ask.

The old man turns to Ashtoreth, ignoring the two of us. I'm two feet away and I can see that his eyes are still milky, but they are focused on her. A smile pulls his wrinkles back, making his face turn cartoonish, like you could pull on his skin and stretch it into any shape you wanted to. There is a devotion in his stare that you only find from lovers.

Or believers.

Ashtoreth reaches up and pats his face. "Thank you for the transport, Chester of Mayfield."

"Anything I can ever do for you I will, Mistress."

"And your worship will be rewarded."

"Your pleasure is the only reward I seek."

"Then your quest is done; you have found it in your service."

She leans in and kisses him.

It starts chaste, two sets of lips pressed gently together, and stays that way for a long moment. Then Ashtoreth's part, opening around Chester's, and he grunts as her tongue slithers out over his and fills his mouth. His milky eyes roll back into his skull under parchment-thin eyelids that flutter like spastic moths. His knees fold and he slides down, down, down, slowly, so, so slowly, to the ground, guided by Ashtoreth's hands on each side of his head. Their mouths don't lose contact, her jaw working and working and working as if she is drinking his insides. The air around them goes coppery and I taste the ozone crackle of her magick on the back of my teeth.

Watching them pulls a shiver out of my body, a betrayal of how I *want* to feel, dispassionate and aloof, separated from them completely, and a tell for how this display is *actually* affecting me. Sweat forms in the hollows of my elbows and the backs of my knees to halfway up my hamstrings.

I can't see him from focusing on Ashtoreth and Chester, but I *hear* Javier breathing like he just ran ten miles, the air drawing deep into his lungs and jerking out immediately in a *whuff.*

I want to say something, order her to stop, but I can't. I'm caught, tangled, trapped and wrapped and enveloped in a web of fascination.

Finally, *she* breaks the kiss, pulling back and pulling away. Tendrils of wet string between her lips and his as if their skin has melted, two sticks of taffy in the warm sun going liquid and melding, blending, swirling into each other to become one skin, one flesh, one meat.

Chester stares up at the Whore Goddess with wide, unfocused eyes that have gone clear like those of a much younger man.

She giggles and the hold on me snaps as if I've been doused with ice water and my sweaty knees go weak and threaten to throw me to the cement under my feet. I feel funny, a clenching strangeness in my pelvis. I'm hot, flushed, and hyper-aware of the sun streaming down on the black coat across my shoulders.

Ashtoreth's smile is crooked. "Thank you for the compliment, Charlie."

"I didn't say anything."

"You don't have to." She tilts her head toward Javier. "He didn't either." Javier has turned away, glancing back at us over his shoulder.

His skin is flushed darker and his shoulders drawn tight around his chest.

Oh.

.

.

.

Oh.

21

CHESTER'S GONE.

After the kiss he stood up, dusted himself off, got in his truck, and drove off.

Ashtoreth and I are sitting at a picnic table under a covering. She lounges on the bench seat, sprawling back over the tabletop where I sit. I've dropped the coat off my shoulders and just have it under me and across my lap. It shifted and shuffled until it settled into place like some kind of pet, cooing the entire time in my head until it got comfortable and then going quiet.

Good.

Javier is off to the restrooms.

I am *not* thinking about that.

The heat is less under the covering but still feels solid against my skin. Yellow jackets buzz around us, landing on the table near a sticky spot that is probably dried soda. They crawl around one another, picking up sugar on their legs. I don't know if they are eating it, gathering it, or rubbing it on their little yellow and black segmented bodies, but I watch them move, focusing on them to keep from focusing on the heat.

The South, man, sticky hot like you've been baked inside a cinnamon roll.

The bees.

A lot of insects crawl over one another and knock one another around in a situation like this, as if they were little drunk psychopaths in a mosh pit of sugar frenzy, but the wasps are careful, barely brushing against one another, acting as if this were a cotillion or a high-society ball with complicated courting dances that require no physical contact save for the touching of fingertips.

"They feel less than that," Ashtoreth says.

Her words make no sense.

"Come again?" I say, and the second I do I wish I could choose other words. She's a love goddess gone to seed and I brace myself for the dirty innuendo.

Ashtoreth doesn't take the opportunity.

Instead her face takes on a mild intensity. "Humans are foolish and shortsighted and myopic and egotistical and ignorant."

"I agree with that, but hey!"

"Your kind continue seeking out the Old Ones, the elder gods, the Great Ones, and others, beseeching them, trying to draw them forth. They think that if they free them then the gods will come here and bless them, give them power as faithful servants after remaking your world."

"I don't do that."

She acts as if I didn't speak. "They don't realize that every time they perform some ritual, some summoning, some *work*, they actually *draw* power from the gods, weakening them and keeping them imprisoned. If they simply left them be, forgot about them, then they would grow in power until they could free themselves from the prison your ancestors' ancestors sent them to so long ago."

"Sounds like an ingenious way to keep them locked up."

"Your ancestors' ancestors meant for their sacrifice to hold.

They had used so much and were not ignorant. They formed the system of their spell wisely."

"What did they sacrifice?"

"The whole world. They flooded the earth and drowned all the worshipers of the Old Ones under the waters of the Deluge save a handful in a bucket."

I laugh even though this isn't funny. I don't know what else to do, what reaction to have. "Let me guess, the main guy's name was Noah."

She looks at me, face blank with seriousness.

"Noach was one of those chosen by Bar-Japeth and the priest-ess 'Adataneses, but *they* were the orchestrators of the flood. Their circle of Sedeqetelebab, Shem, Ne'elatama'uk, and Ham harnessed the life force of the dead and dying to expel the Old Ones to the other side of this universe."

"Wait." I can't believe what I am hearing. It's so absurd I have to ask, "Noah's ark was real?"

"Noach?" She laughs. "Noach wasn't the builder of the vessel. Emzana was."

"Who?"

"His lover, also the one who encouraged Noach to use his tal-ent for storytelling to take credit for it all in the raw aftermath."

I mull over what she just told me. I didn't grow up religious. My town was, my parents are, but it never took with me, espe-cially after . . . that night (because if God exists then fuck Him for letting that happen to me), but I have a handle on the basics. I was taken to Sunday school enough to know Noah and his ark and the flood and the animals.

Wait.

Am I religious now?

Maybe. I don't know. I now have irrefutable proof that things that are not human exist. I have met and fought gods and their minions. I have fucking magick in my blood. Hell, I am sitting six inches from a fallen goddess of love.

But religious?

Maybe.

I don't know.

Don't ask me to pray for you.

"If they banished all the gods, how did you get here?" I ask.

"Child, I never left."

"I don't know what that means."

She draws a long breath in. "I was born in the mud beneath my mother. I crawled out of the muck fully formed and without void as the woman who gave birth to me lay cooling in the rain. My father loomed over us, his body blocking even the meager sun that tried to break the gray slate of the sky above. I knelt in his shadow as he stared down and waited for him to lift me up and claim me as his child."

She stops talking and I wait. Even in the heat I can feel the ancient chill of her birthplace inside my skin.

It's a long moment before she speaks again.

"He turned away and left me there in the mud between the thighs of my mother's corpse. I wasn't his child; I was simply his seed planted and sprung to life. Not worth his notice, much less his love."

A tear tracks down her cheek and as I watch it slide over her skin I feel the hollow ache of abandonment in the marrow of my bones.

"I stayed there until I could bear no more. I rose and walked into the world seeking the thing I had been denied.

"At first I was full of wrath. I burned and raged and tore lovers apart by their roots and sowed strife and discord and infidelity. I crushed dreams and destroyed souls until I gained the maturity to understand that the thing I sought to destroy was the thing I sought for myself. Since then, I find and foment love. Emzana bound me to the timbers of her ark, knowing I would be needed, and I hung there through the storm, baptized in the wrath of their working. I was there with Shem and Ham as they burned with desire for each other even though they were brothers. I was there to encourage 'Adataneses to seduce Sedeqetelebab and bring her to Bar-Japeth. I rode in the vessel and lived on all the love that was there. Without me your race would have died in those days. I survived the Deluge and the outing that followed because I never left."

One thought rolled through my mind.

Lady, you are really fucked up.

What I said was, "Why tell me all of this?"

"We are friends, Charlie. Don't friends share their pain and their secrets?"

Something sarcastic rises up in me, the same sarcasm I use so often in defense. Not like a shield but like a bludgeon, a preemptive strike to keep me safe.

I bite it back and say, "Yes, Ashtoreth, we are."

She smiles and it's actually beautiful. "Call me Ash, if you want. I always wanted someone to call me that."

Her voice is . . . so . . . soft, so childlike it hurts.

"Okay, Ash. Anything you want."

Goddessdamn.

22

———

JAVIER IS HOLDING the bottom hem of his shirt in his hand, forming a pouch that has weird shapes poking through the thin cloth. Tiny beads of sweat cling to the fine hairs on his arms and the back edge of his jawline. He steps to the table and drops the hem of his shirt.

There is a jumble tumble of bright wrappers and bottles that spills out on the table making the yellow-jackets buzz away.

Snacks. He bought snacks.

Looking at them, I realize my stomach is in a knot and my eyes won't leave a package of peanut butter cups.

"I was hungry. Figured you would be too." He sits down and waves his arm over the pile. "You pick first."

I snatch up the candy I was looking at and begin peeling it apart. The chocolate has gone soft and sticky against the inside of the wrapper and the second I perforate the thin Mylar I smell warm peanuts.

I can't shove them into my mouth fast enough.

The first cup smears the top of my tongue and glues

itself to the roof of my mouth. I pick up a soda and drink, the carbonated water breaking it free so I can swallow.

"How long were we in that truck?"

Ashtoreth shrugs. "Long enough for the moon to hide and the sun to search for her."

Javier looks at me. "How long is that?"

I shrug. "She doesn't have a watch apparently."

Ashtoreth sniffs. "Time is mostly inconsequential."

Javier swallows some candy-coated chocolate. "Why does the moon hide from the sun?"

"She wants to ravish him."

He looks at me again. "Is she serious?"

I pick up another candy bar, something with toffee under the chocolate that is silky warm across my mouth. "Probably."

Ashtoreth turns and looks at him straight on. "The sun's love is too rough for the moon. She doesn't respect his boundaries and the pain makes him run and hide. He is wolf to her rabbit."

"That makes no sense, *chica*."

"I know." The look on Ashtoreth's face is sad. "She would do better to listen to his needs and seduce rather than chase. If she catches him she would make the effort to break him to her will and he knows this to be true. But rabbits are vicious and cannot help their nature; a wolf can only run." Ashtoreth frowns and her eyes go all somber. "It will not end well."

I screw the cap on my soda. I can see Javier is going to keep chasing this conversation and after the Noah thing I just can't listen to it. "Ash, I need your help."

She turns to me. "We are friends."

"I know." *This is so weird.*

"How can I help you?"

"I can't find the Man in Black."

"Oh, Charlie." Her eyes go big and her mouth forms a circle. "Why would you want to?"

"I need to."

She looks at me and I *feel* her gaze change as I watch it in her irises. They crackle and flash from burnt-honey brown to a blue so pure it hurts behind my breastbone. She's using whatever her version of Sight is on me.

I want to lash out, hit and scream and run, to stop her. *Don't use magick on me. Don't fucking do it!*

Stop. Hold it together. She's supposed to be your friend.

Friend.

I sit and let her Look.

After a moment she blinks and her eyes fade back to their darker colour. "You've broken your connection to him."

"I did."

"And my torc does not work to find him?"

"I've looked for weeks, hunting down all kinds of creatures that even smelled of him"—*in sewers and alleys and deserts and even a swamp*—"and I have nothing. Finally, one of them said your name to help find a hidden god."

"If someone as powerful as Nyarlathotep hides themselves, then even I cannot find them."

The edge creeps into my voice unbidden, but I don't fight it. "That thing lied to me then and this is a waste of my time."

I push off the table. The coat clings to my waist, slithering with me.

"Hold, Charlie." Ashtoreth rises and her hand snags an edge of the coat. It makes a noise in my head that sounds as close to a bark as its alien melody can.

"Let go."

She does. "There is one thing."

"What?"

"If I had something of his, something of his nature still connected to him, then I could follow that link back no matter where he is."

I think about it and hold out my hand, showing my Mark. "He did this to me."

She shakes her head. "You broke that connection."

I reach in and pull out the black-bladed katana. Javier jumps up from the table as it slides out. "Where was that?"

"It's magick, Javier."

His eyes trace around the blade as the sunlight gleams along the razored edge. "Can I hold it?"

The sword is hungry. It swells against my Mark like a living thing instead of a forged weapon. What would it do to an un-magicked, unMarked human who picked it up? For a dark second I am tempted to hand it over, to see what would happen. Would it drain the life from Javier? Would it make him turn the sword on himself, to commit seppuku here by the highway? Would it drive him insane and make him lash out, to use the sword to cut Ashtoreth and me down?

"No."

I realize we are still in the open in a public place. This is a rest stop. People, normal people, stop here. Families on vacation, truckers just trying to make a dollar, people homeless by choice and circumstance all could be here.

And I'm standing here in the open holding a cursed sword as if it were nothing.

I lower the blade and look around.

There are people in the rest area, not many and none close. Nobody is looking directly at us, but suddenly I feel like a clock is ticking and that the state patrol has been contacted and is heading here now to gun down the crazy woman with a sword.

This pressure makes my voice come harshly from between clenched teeth. "Will this work? It was his."

"Oathbreaker is aptly named. They can be possessed but never owned. The Son of Azathoth held them as you do now, but they were never his."

Dammit.

I drop the blade back into the coat.

The minute my fingers let go of the handle they begin to tingle and ache in the first knuckle.

Javier makes a small noise as it sinks from sight.

Ashtoreth bites her lip. "Do not be too casual with Oathbreaker. They are a treacherous thing."

"I'll take it under advisement."

Do I hear sirens?

In the distance it sounds like a wail, undulating, like sirens coming fast.

I look around and everyone is still meandering around the area as they were. No one is driving away; no one is looking over.

But I can't shake the feeling.

Would the state patrol use sirens to respond?

"Can you think of anything else that Nyarlathotep could be connected to?" Ashtoreth asks.

I move my mouth to answer her, but my words are trapped behind a wall in my brain. I can't think about anything else but the impending showdown with the police.

"Are you okay, Charlie?" Javier asks.

Those *are* sirens.

The police are coming.

The coat rustles, drawing tight around me, binding me, and I pull against it with a snarl.

My hand moves, rising, reaching in, and my head is full of the vision of me pulling the sword out again and standing my ground.

The police would fall like wheat before the scythe, cut down in a spray of hot blood and a rush of intestine spilling from split-open bodies. Hearts still beating would shower me with iron-tinged life and I would drink my fill.

The world has washed crimson across my eyes.

I smell the insides of my prey. My mouth runs at the corners and I want and hunger and thirst for it.

.

.

.

My brain is cut in half by the sharp, clear sound of a ringing bell.

23

THE SOUND BANGS into the bones of my temples, vibrating along the sutures of my skull. It tumbles down the zigs and the zags of them and makes the blood-soaked sponge that is my brain itch. The chime sings into my sinuses in a vibrato that makes my eyeteeth go cold and achy. My eyes are pressed so tightly together with it that all I can see is an orange burst from the compression of my eyeball against the optic nerve. I stumble and fall against something that is soft and hard and wraps around me as I fall.

A warm, wet sound *chuffs* beside my ear.

The ringing fades, pulsing into a soft buzz in the center of the nerve bundle tucked around my top vertebra.

I can open my eyes. I'm sitting on my ass beside the picnic table. Ashtoreth stands over me, rimmed in white sunlight.

"You okay, Charlie?"

The voice is near my ear.

And male.

I jerk and find Javier sitting behind me. My brain is too numb to jolt into panic at his nearness. His legs splay on each side of me. He must have tried to catch me when I fell backward.

"Fine. I'm fine." I grab the bench and pull myself up. My head is clear. "What happened?"

Javier climbs to his feet. "She thumped that thing around your neck."

Ashtoreth shrugs. "I warned you to be careful with Oathbreaker."

"I've been using that sword for weeks. I've felt it wanting *more* and never wanting me to put it up, but nothing like that." The wash of bloodthirst still lingers but just on the edges. Why did the sword affect me like that?

Ashtoreth sits on the table, chewing her thumbnail and looking away.

"Ash?"

She tears a thin strip of cuticle off with her teeth and spits it away. "We are friends, Charlie."

Wait a minute.

"You affected it. You made it turn on me."

She sighs and I feel it all the way down to my diaphragm. "I am still a goddess of desire. It's why you want to be my friend. Oathbreaker is a creature of desire. They are nothing but want and need and thirst." She goes back to chewing her thumbnail, talking around it. "It is my nature that made them stronger, more focused, but it is a side effect. I did not betray you with them."

I watch her.

She looks small, younger than before. Like a fifteen-year-old girl not ready for the big bad world. It's a lie. I know who she is. I know *what* she is. She's one of the reasons it's a big bad world.

Maybe not a lie, but this version of her isn't the truth.

She is a lie.

But is she lying?

Gods, who fucking knows? All of a sudden I'm tired again.

Tired of the tension of waiting to be fucked over by something not even human. Can I trust a millennium-old goddess of whores?

Probably not.

But here goes nothing.

"I believe you."

Light explodes across her face in a smile. "We really are friends, aren't we?"

"We are."

Javier coughs.

I sigh. "Hell, Javi, I'll throw you in too."

He grins as big as Ashtoreth. When did my friendship become so damn desirable?

"What did you think of before Oathbreaker made their move against you?" Ashtoreth asks.

"I know someone connected to the Man in Black."

She looks at me expectantly.

"Daniel."

"Ah, the dark-haired minion. Yes, he would do."

"He's not a minion anymore," I say. "Not the Man in Black's anyway."

She smiles. "You claimed him for yourself?"

I squirm under the presumption. "Not exactly."

"He would have been easy for you to woo away from the Prince of Darkness."

"Wait," Javier says.

I turn to him.

"How many people are we hunting?"

"One."

"One?" His eyebrows are touching. "He has more than one name?"

Ashtoreth laughs. "Child, he has more names than you could speak if you said them and nothing else for the rest of your life."

Javier looks from her to me.

I shrug. "I know."

"Who are we after?"

"Nyarlathotep. He's a god of chaos and destruction. I usually call him the Man in Black, but he also goes by the Crawling Chaos, the Prince of Nightmares or Darkness, and his name."

"Why so many nicknames?"

"They are titles. One thing I've learned, the bigger the god you are up against, the more titles they go by."

"How do you keep up?"

I shrug. "You just do. It just falls into a rhythm."

"So just roll with it?"

"Just roll with it."

He nods and steps back.

"What were you saying about Daniel?" I ask Ashtoreth.

"Only that you could pull him from the Lord of Darkness"— from the corner of my eye I see Javier gesture as he caught the new title—"without a large struggle."

"Why would you say that?"

"His heart was already divided between you."

"What?"

"Oh please, child"—she rolls her eyes—"that boy loved you. I know about these things."

Daniel met the Man in Black the same night I did and immediately fell under his sway. Daniel had become mine after I cut him free from a life force–siphoning cancer god, but in the process I discovered that my magick was using him as a battery. I ended that, but he was still magickally connected to me.

No, that isn't why I love him or why he loves me.

I mean . . .

Shut up.

Ashtoreth frowns. "If he is yours he will not be connected to his old master."

"The Man in Black took his soul."

"Oh." She taps her chin, thinking. "That may work. Take us to him."

The thought of wishing somewhere makes my energy drop like a stone down an empty well. "I was hoping you could do that for me."

"I don't have that ability."

I touch the torc around my throat. "Didn't I get that from you? I couldn't do that before you gave me this."

She laughs. "You had no aim before my gift to you. I didn't grant you travel, merely the ability to choose a destination."

Shit.

Ashtoreth claps her hands and smiles widely. "If I had such ability do you think I would ride in a truck driven by a worshiper? I don't like your talk radio that much."

Javier says, "You shouldn't like it at all."

She turns to him. "Why should you presume to tell me what I should and should not enjoy?"

He shrugs, not looking at her. "Just full of racist homophobes, that's all."

"Do you not find ignorance amusing?"

"Nah, shit ain't funny, senorita."

Ashtoreth moves over to him and climbs up on the table to sit next to him. Her body and his touch in a long line of leg, hip, and shoulder. For a brief moment I want to shift my magick and open my Sight, to See her horrific, alien true form contrasted against his humanity. It feels like something that would be in an absurd horror comedy: She's a fallen whore goddess! He's an angsty young human! Watch as hijinks ensue!

But I don't.

I keep my magick firmly where it is and just watch them in their human forms.

"Javier," she says, "your species are nothing; you aren't even a blink of eternity's eye; you may be the impulse to blink the same way a mote of dust can cause your eye to twitch. While you are alive you spend your first decade in ignorance and your last in senility. In between you have an entire universe that you know of conspiring against you, seeking to snuff your candle. You have a body that will betray you. Now you, Javier, also know that there are things beyond the darkness that also seek your destruction." Her arm slips around his shoulders. "In all of *that* there are humans, the majority of you in fact, who waste their time arguing about how some of you are different from the others because of your skin colour, where you were born, or who you want to mate with. How can you not find that utterly hilarious?"

"She has a point," I say.

"Yeah"—he nods—"still feels wrong when they're talking about you."

Ashtoreth frowns. "I did not consider it from that perspective."

Javier shrugs under her arm. "No biggie."

Quick as a serpent she darts in and kisses him on the cheek.

My body goes tense.

Javier leans away, his cheeks gone dark with blush. I watch through narrow eyes, waiting to see if anything happens, but it doesn't.

It appears to be just lips on skin, simply a kiss on a cheek.

I guess I don't trust Ashtoreth after all.

She places her chin on his shoulder and breathes her words against his face. "It has been a long time since I learned something about you humans. Thank you, Javier."

He blushes. He actually blushes.

It's . . . sweet.

I bite my tongue to not remind him of her true form.

After a long moment, she sits back and turns to me. "Now you have to do what you have to do."

"What does that mean?"

"You have to take us to your Daniel."

I shake my head. "I don't have it in me."

I truly don't. I feel better than I did, but if I wished all three of us across the country right now I'd turn inside out.

Stop that line of thought.

"Use the tool you brought," she says.

What?

Before I can ask she slowly tilts her head sideways toward Javier. Oh.

"No." The word comes out sharp, harsher than I intended.

She frowns, her bottom lip curling out. "You brought him here."

"Not for that. Never for that."

"Now, child, you are simply being stubborn."

My face goes tight, the ache setting up in the back of my teeth where they clench. "Not. Going. To. Happen." Warm magick bubbles into my chest.

Javier slides off the table. "What's going on?"

I don't say anything, trying to calm down.

Ashtoreth isn't having that struggle. "She is refusing to do what is necessary."

"What's that?" he asks.

"No," I say.

Ashtoreth ignores me and keeps talking. "We need to travel to Daniel's side—"

"Who's that?" he interrupts.

"Her *paramour.*"

Something about her inflection of the word makes my cheeks burn. "We've never . . ." I stop speaking, not wanting to share personal information.

"I don't know that word," Javier says to Ashtoreth.

"Her lover." I don't try to correct her again and she keeps talking. "We need to go where he is; time is a factor."

"She can just zap us there."

"She has expended her magick. She doesn't have it in her to spell us from here to there. She must have your help."

He stands up straighter. "Anything she needs."

Enough of this. "Javier, you don't know what you are saying."

"I'm part of your crew, Charlie. I'm not here to look around; I'm here to work. If you need me to do something I'll do it."

"I don't have a crew."

"You've got me and her and, apparently, this Daniel guy. And I think your coat is alive, so it might be part of the crew too. That's a thing."

The coat rustles in agreement to his words, filling my head with its cooing.

Hush.

The coat falls silent.

A crew.

It sounds weird in my head. People who choose to follow me? What?

I've been alone most of my life. In some ways what Tyler and *his* crew did when I was fourteen killed me. My body went on, but it was years, hard-fought and hard-won *years,* of therapy and martial arts and pain until I could live again. A lot of that time was spent separated from people, in the same room, the same public places, the same dojo as them, but always apart, always shielded in pain and anger and isolation. Even from my family who love me. I know now that my mom and dad had a tremendous load of guilt over my assault, pain of their own because I, their child, had suffered that, and anger at their own feelings of inadequacy and helplessness. They weren't prepared to handle that on top of my pain and anger, such furious anger that I had no choice but to pour it out in the only safe haven I knew. And I was so hurt and so young, left broken and raw and destroyed but still alive to scream and cry through the pain of even living each day afterward, that I couldn't articulate, couldn't just tell them why I did the things I did, why I lashed out at them when they were trying their best.

And so I was alone even with them.

Separated from the world around me until the scar tissue finally softened and I met Daniel.

He found me, not healed but healed *enough,* and he was patient and kind and understanding and in his grace I finally found someone I could let in.

And so now the idea of people choosing to be with me, to *follow* me, is alien and strange. And it chafes.

"Why?" I ask.

"You saved me from doing something dumb," Javier says.

"You're my friend," Ashtoreth says.

The coat whispers in my head that I set it free.

Well, I'll be damned.

Okay.

"What do I do? How do I do this with Javier?"

Ashtoreth tilts her head, looking at me like an owl confused by the field mouse. "You do the same thing that connected you to your lover."

Her choice of words, the tone of her voice, and the look on her face make me pause. "Wait, what do you think Daniel and I did?"

The word that spills from her mouth isn't even human, much less English. It rolls off her tongue and hangs in the air between us, entwining on itself and rubbing syllable against syllable, consonants entering vowels, diphthongs squeezing and constricting. The word *throbs* at me and I feel it like a pulse against my skin and inside me, deep inside, there is an answering beat that nearly takes my breath away.

From the side, Javier says soft and low: "Whoa."

Whoa is right.

"We didn't do *that*," I say. "I'm not even sure what *that* is and if humans could do that."

She chuckles. "You can, but it is not for the faint of heart."

I take a step back.

Sexuality, my sexuality, confuses me. It just does. I walled it off for so long after what happened that it still feels somehow dangerous. It took years of therapy to even talk about it and years more to separate it from the trauma and it still isn't a clean break, it is messy and jumbled and some days more and some days less and logically, in my brain, I know that it's kind of that way for everyone, even people who didn't suffer violation or abuse.

But it feels like I am a freak sometimes.

I put my hand up. "Don't screw with me, Ashtoreth. Just tell me the most . . . I don't know what word I'm looking for."

"*Platonic*?" Javier supplies.

"Yes." I nod at him in thanks. "The most platonic way to use Javier to power my magick."

"Out loud it sounds weird," Javier says.

"It does," I agree.

"Not to me," Ashtoreth says.

Javier and I look at each other and I know we both have the same thought: *Your version of weird is way further out there than ours.*

"Silly, reticent humans." She sighs deep inside her lungs.

I shrug. "That's us. Now what do I do?"

"Kiss him."

Javier and I look at each other.

"That's the only way?"

"No. But it is the most *platonic* way I know."

"Is that because you're a"—I stop myself before using the word *whore*—"love goddess?"

Her eyes turn up as she thinks about it. "Mayhaps."

"Well, I guess we don't have anyone to ask a second opinion of," I say. Oh god. I've only ever kissed one person. "You okay with this, Javier?"

It takes him a long moment to reply. "Yeah."

Neither one of us moves.

Ashtoreth is smiling when she says:

"I thought time was of the essence."

24

———————

WE ARE FACE-TO-FACE less than a foot apart.

I could touch him by barely moving and he could touch me, but we just stand looking at each other. He's sweating. Not profusely, but a light glistening across his forehead. He has nice eyes. They hold shadows in them, but they're a warm brown, like roasted chestnuts or good coffee.

He's not bad looking, but my brain immediately begins comparing him to Daniel. Daniel's broader chin, the slight crook of his nose from being broken, the bright emerald of his eyes and their tiny gold flecks.

The only person I've ever kissed.

Now it would be two.

It is just a kiss.

Just a kiss.

Why does it feel like so much more than that? Will it be more than that? I know my magick can make someone into my slave. I do *not* want that with Javier. Not at all.

Immediately I wish I had ditched him when I wanted to before. Then this wouldn't even be an option or a risk. He'd be safe. Instead I am going to pull him deeper into this world of bloodthirsty gods who want to devour us all.

I can't.

I won't.

"Hey," he says, "it's okay. We can do this." His hands close on the sleeves of the coat and it sings out. It pulls across the backs of my knees as its hem moves forward to caress along Javier's legs. The coat likes him.

I look into his eyes and there is a determination there. He's in this thing already. He's been magicked across the country by me. He watched me fight the sand dweller. He's seen Ashtoreth's true form.

And he's down to ride.

Okay.

Fuck it.

I reach up and his hands fall away from my arms. The skin on his face is smooth and warm under my palms as I pull his mouth to mine.

Our lips press together.

It's . . . awkward. I can feel his teeth hard on the other side of thin lips, the fuzz of his baby mustache tickles my nose, and his breath is hot and moist in one small spot to the side of my nose.

And there's nothing.

No spark.

No connection.

No thrill.

Just two faces smushed together.

I feel him start to pull away.

As I pull him closer, my lips part against his and he yields to me, opening to me. My tongue slides into his mouth and there is a *click* at the back of my skull and my brain begins to rattle and hum and I feel Javier in my hands as if his skull is a cup I can drink from. His life force pours down my throat and it's thin and sharp like I think wine would taste and undercut with a herbal bitterness that only feeds my thirst for it. I swallow his energy down and it hits my magick like a cup of high-octane gasoline thrown on a fire.

The magick erupts, filling my body as it lights my blood on fire and paints the backs of my eyelids with white static. I could drain him, take all of his life and keep it in my belly. He would let me. He is limp in my hands, not moving, not fighting.

I could have him all.

I would never want again if I simply drink him down.

I push away from the lie of that thought and him away from me. The connection remains, stretched between us, but now I can think. The want to drain him is an echo instead of all I can hear. I concentrate and squeeze the connection shut. Javier sways on his feet but doesn't fall. His eyes are glassy and his smile is slack. His lips still glisten with my saliva.

Understanding slides into my head. My magick is triggered mostly by contact with bodily fluid. That's why the kiss worked so well.

I feel light and tight, magick tingling under my skin. The world around looks sharper, brighter.

Ashtoreth is smiling.

"Feeling better?" she asks.

Before I can say it Javier responds. "Oh *yeah, mamacita.*"

25

WE DROP OUT of the etheric realm, swirl to a stop on slick hospital tile, and I grab Javier around the shoulders. He feels thin and is already starting to shake. The room is dark, only illuminated by dim lights in a panel behind the bed in the center, the soft glowing displays of machinery that softly beeps and clicks and whirrs, and the spill of butter yellow light from under the door.

The room is exactly how I remember it from weeks ago.

Javier puts his hand to his mouth and his shoulders buck under my arm. I give him a push toward the bathroom and he stumbles that way, grabbing the doorframe and pulling himself inside as if the room had tilted up on end and he had to haul himself in or fall to his death. Light rolls out of the open door and then it shuts behind him and I hear the wet honking of Javier losing his stomach into the toilet.

Not so much with the *mamacita* shit now.

Even just using a smidge of his life force to teleport us he's going to be feeling it for a while.

I stay facing the door to leave the room.

Ashtoreth looks at me. "How long has it been since you've been here?"

"It's been a while."

"Face your fear, Charlie."

"I'm not afraid."

"It is naked on your face."

"That's just my face. It looks like that."

"Charlie, turn around."

I do.

Daniel lies on the bed, covers pulled up over his chest. I move over to him and Ashtoreth follows. Daniel looks peaceful, sleeping, but he's not.

He's in a coma.

A tube circles his face, pushed into his nose, and more tubes and wires run from him to the bank of machinery on the side of the bed. They look like a tangled mess, knotted up and twisted, but I guess they do what they are supposed to. The machines just keep beeping and humming along. He's thinner, his cheekbones sharp as razors, his brow and chin showing more than they used to, and his eyes have dark circles around them.

But it's still Daniel.

Still the face I fell in love with. Under those waxy lids are still the green eyes I fell into with trust and hope to not be hurt again. Those lips are on the mouth that laughs so full and rich and wholeheartedly that it makes you smile until you feel it all the way down into your chest.

My chest.

Right now my chest feels like a closed fist and my eyes are hot and if I blink tears will push out of them. I'm angry, angry all over again. This is the Man in Black's fault. He did this.

"Do the thing," I say to Ashtoreth. "Track down that son of a bitch so I can kill him."

She doesn't move.

I turn toward her.

Her mouth is turned down, her eyes soft. "Charlie . . ." Her voice trails away, but I can hear the excuse underneath it.

The anger flares inside me. "Don't."

"I'm sorry but—"

The anger roars. "No *buts*. Don't give me any *sorrys* and don't you *dare* say any *buts*."

"He is no longer connected to Nyarlathotep. I cannot use him."

"*Shut your lying mouth!*" I scream. I want to smash her face in. My fists clench at the ends of my arms and I want to drive them through the back of her skull. The coat goes hard around me, forming spikes of darkness along my shoulders and arms. Ashtoreth cringes and I see the fear in her eyes. It's raw and naked and the sight of it makes the rage in me surge.

I push off the bed rail and throw myself back before I can tear her limb from limb.

Spinning away, I stalk to the door, seething. Javier comes out of the bathroom and I shove him out of my way, slamming him against the wall. My hand falls on the door handle and I feel like I could rip it off the hinges. I have to go, I have to leave, or I *am* going to hurt someone. Yanking the door open, I stalk out into the hospital hallway.

And come face-to-face with the skinhound snarling and dripping saliva on the gleaming white hospital tile.

I feel my lips pull back on my face so hard it hurts.

Not a smile, but a snarl of my own to match.

Boy, did you pick the wrong time for this, Fido.

26

THE DOOR SHUSHES closed behind me. The wide hospital
hallway is empty and dim, the lights taken on a blue-
greenish underwater tone. Shadows gather along the
ceiling and where the walls meet the floor, giving the
entire scene a filtered effect. Everything looks off,
slightly stretched and coated in dirty Vaseline.

There's spooky shit happening.

I spent nearly two weeks in this hospital at Daniel's
side before leaving on this . . . mission. It's a busy med-
ical center in the downtown of a major U.S. city. There
was always someone around. Nurses, people visiting
their loved ones, pastors giving comfort, janitors mop-
ping, doctors on rounds.

Now the place feels empty.

As if me and the otherworldly monster in front of me
are encapsulated in our own little bubble of unreality.

I feel the spell the second I recognize its effect.

The skinhound cocks his head, looking at me with
the one eye he has left, the one eye I had left him

with. Loose slabs of raw muscle vibrate on his shoulders and chest as he growls low and long through clenched teeth. The noise of it rolls down the hallway, rumbling against my skin. Strings of ichor hang from his jaws, swaying to and fro, to and fro, to and fro until one breaks and slings down to splat on the floor.

The coat ruffles around me, the hem of it stretching along the floor and spreading to make me look bigger than I am.

You would think in a situation like this it would be singing in my head, but it doesn't. When the shit gets real the coat shuts up and lets me work.

I reach inside it. It tightens around my arm, slowing me just a touch. I'm reaching into the left inside pocket. The one with the sword. I know what happened earlier, but I don't care right now.

Right this minute me and Oathbreaker will see eye to eye.

27

THE SWORD PULLS free from the darkness of the coat in one smooth motion, chiming out as if released from a scabbard. The feel of the handle against my Mark gives me a surge of energy and I feel stronger with it in my hand. More confident. More capable. I sweep the black blade in a semi-circle to hear it slice the air around me. Its thirst comes pouring down my arm, making my throat tighten in anticipation, but it's like it was before Ashtoreth. There, but not driving. I am in control. Perfect control.

Don't get cocky; cocky gets you hurt.

I hear that in the Irish honey rasp of Sensei Laura.

She'd say it to me right before doing something that put me on my back tapping the mat in submission or trying to desperately pull air back into lungs that somehow had stopped working.

Or coming to from something I never saw happen.

But Sensei Laura never had a living, cursed sword.

Or magick.

So I push her voice out of my head.

At the sight of the sword the skinhound barks and takes a step back. It's a strangled sound, asthmatic and wheezing. It surprises me. Weeks of being followed by this damn thing and I've never heard him do anything other than growl. Usually he is silent.

"Oh, you don't like that?" I snarl. "Imagine how much you aren't going to like it when I cut you in two."

The skinhound yips and lowers himself on raw haunches.

Then he steps forward again.

The sword sings out, its thirst pulsing down my arm and spilling into my chest. My stomach clenches in response. I pull the sword up by my face in ready position and feel heat radiating off the razor edge of it. I growl back at the skinhound. "One more step."

He launches himself at me in an oily uncoiling of vivisected muscle.

Ripping the sword around, I swing for his thick neck. As the blade curves through the air at the end of my arm I can already *feel* it slicing through the muscle, cutting the fiber of it, shearing through the vertebrae hidden inside, and my heart surges in my chest with the thought of one blow one kill.

A split second before the edge of the sword can connect, the skinhound twists in midair.

He rolls around my strike like liquid mercury, his body defying the laws of physics, and his teeth clamp on to my left arm. The coat screams as the long teeth punch through it, but it still hardens around my arm, protecting me. The skinhound's momentum whips his body through the air, jerking me around and off my feet. I hit the tile hard, landing on my chest and chin, mostly my chin. The jolt cracks my teeth together and sends flashes of bright white crashing against my eyelids. Oathbreaker clatters out of my hand, bouncing away, leaving me unarmed.

I open my eyes, lying on my stomach, and they are full of water, making everything blurry and indistinct. I can make out the shape of the skinhound as he struggles to catch purchase on the hospital tile.

Get up. Get up or get dead! Sensei Laura screams in my head.

Pushing into a roll, I sit up and shake my head, trying to clear it out. The blow to my chin rung my bell and now everything is in sight, but it all has a vibration to it, making it slightly indistinct, as if I am out of sync with the frequency of the world around me. Climbing to my feet, I look for Oathbreaker but don't see it.

The *clickity-clack* of nails on tile brings me back to the skinhound.

He's coming at me, trotting down the hallway, building momentum. I drop down, lowering my stance, getting ready for him. My arm is throbbing from the pressure of the bite and my shoulder has a white-hot needle of pain jabbing into it from being yanked around.

And everything is still fuzzy.

And I don't care.

The adrenaline sings in my blood, making my body tingle. Magick bubbles in my stomach and spills out of my Mark in crimson gobbets of etheric energy. I feel electrified and in this moment I am alive, nothing more, only alive, and nothing matters but me and my enemy.

In this moment there is no Man in Black, no elder gods with bad intentions, no Daniel being in a coma.

Just war.

The skinhound hits me dead center, weighing more than me and full of power, but I am ready and braced. My fingers dig into the raw meat of him, sinking like it's gelatin. I twist with my hips and thrust with my legs, taking the skinhound off his feet. The coat whips up around me, slapping into the skinhound and helping me lift as I toss the damned thing up and over my shoulder and away from me.

He crashes into the ceiling with a yelp, knocking white acoustic tiles down in a shower of dust and dirt. He slams into a light fixture and the fluorescent bulbs explode on impact, tinkling down onto the tile in a shower of tiny glass shards. The skinhound lands in it, sliding along his side for a few feet. The broken glass sticks to his body but doesn't seem to hurt him at all.

He climbs to his feet, but I'm still on mine. I'm sucking wind, but I'm doing it standing up.

Take that, sucker!

My hands ball into fists; my right one, the one with the Mark, feels swollen and heavy and hot. I glance down and it is nearly twice the size it's supposed to be, the flesh along the back of it tight and veiny and crimson red. Magick leaks out of the sides of it like pus from a suppurated wound.

My red right hand.

I'm still staring at it when the skinhound sinks his teeth on my leg and drags me to the floor.

28

___

I'M BEING SHAKEN, slid across the tiles like a toy. My head bangs against the door to Daniel's room and I get my arms up to protect it. I want to throw my hands out, to stop my movement, but I keep the right one clenched tight and the left stays by my face.

The coat is rolled up under me and I feel it struggling to get out so it can help.

I kick out and my foot hits something solid, but I don't know if it's the wall or the skinhound's shoulder. My other leg screams in pain as the skinhound keeps it in his jaws and lifts his head. I kick again and feel it in my other leg, so I know I hit the skinhound.

The pressure on my leg lets go suddenly and I flop over onto my back. Before I can push and get to my feet the skinhound is up by my chest, jaws snapping. I feel a string of ichor land on my cheek and it stings like chemicals. He tenses above me and I know with all certainty he is about to lunge and tear my throat out.

Come on.

Come *on*!

He lunges and I swing with all my might, driving my magick-laden fist into the side of his raw skull, just behind his bulging jaw and clacking, threshing teeth.

It's like I hit him with a sledgehammer and the strength of ten mighty men.

The skinhound yelps and flips backward, blasted away from me by the magick I unleash. As he falls, a ribbon of etheric energy stretches from my hand to him and I tap my ability, calling on my Mark, and I sink the hook *deep*.

My magick connects with the skinhound and my head rushes with the weird alien landscape that is an otherworldly creature's mind. Nothing makes sense; everything is in fluid feelings and pictures and . . . scents? Yes, even without a nose, skinhounds work off of smell. There's a picture of me wrapped in the scent of un-cooked steak and dry grass.

It takes me a second to get my mind clear. To fight back to human.

The skinhound doesn't attack; he sits on the tile, looking up at me with his one baleful eye and waiting for my command.

The magick stretches between us, sticky like taffy and just as messy, but the connection on each end is solid. It's not a sensation but a concept, like when you drive a car and you know without looking how much space that vehicle occupies around you so that you can move in traffic without causing a crash. You don't feel the car outside of the seat, the wheel, and the pedals, but you know it like you know the end of your own arm. This is like that. The skinhound isn't me but an extension of me and my will, bonded though the magick strung betwixt and between us.

The world narrows, the empty hospital falling away, everything tightening down to just me and this thing that has tracked me, has *hounded* me, since the Man in Black swept through my door and dragged me into a world of elder godly shit.

Holding the connection, I take a step toward the skinhound.

My foot hits something that clatters and chimes, muffled under the hem of the coat. I glance down to find Oathbreaker lying naked and raw at my feet.

For a moment I hesitate, afraid to pick it up, afraid that doing so will break the connection between me and the skinhound. I let my mind slide down the ribbon of etheric energy and test it, tugging on the barb of the spell I've cast. It's deep, sunk into the meat of the creature. He won't be removing it without chewing part of himself off. As I pull to test it the prongs of my magick sink deeper, setting in place. The skinhound whimpers and drops flat, lying in a puddle of his own wet.

I reach down to pick up Oathbreaker and notice that my hand is back to normal. I guess expelling that magick fixed it. It still tingles and aches in the joints, but it looks normal.

Except for the crimson glow of magick.

Oathbreaker feels like it leaps to my fingers when I touch it. They are glad to be back in my hand.

I move to the skinhound, the cursed blade naked in my hand, not gleaming at all in the flickering half-light of the hallway. He looks up at me, lifting his skinless face just enough to roll his one egg yolk eye to look at me.

Oathbreaker pushes against my Mark, urging me to swing it, to cleave this demon dog in two and end his blasphemous existence.

My left ear, the ruined one, the one that's nothing but a gnarl of scar tissue and shredded cartilage, *throbs* as if a cold breeze just blew across it. This skinhound did that to me.

I roll my fingers on Oathbreaker's handle and they pulse in response, eager to be put to their bloody-handed purpose. I lift them over my head, ready to apply them to the task of destroying this thing at my feet.

The skinhound drops his head with a whimper and a squelch.

Then he rolls over and gives me his belly.

Like a real dog.

Like *my* real dog.

My head fills with the memory of Winston, the great shaggy giant of a golden retriever I grew up with. He was huge my whole life, bigger than me by at least fifty pounds, making the earth shake as he would bound joyfully up to me and then drop and roll to his back, legs akimbo in the air, belly exposed for rubbing, like a giant fool. He did this every time he would see me whether it had been five minutes or five days. After the thing happened, after I had come home from the hospital, he had sensed I was hurt and when he dropped and rolled it was slowly, gently, so he wouldn't hurt me more or spook me, but still showing me he loved me. He moved into my bedroom after that, sleeping beside me each night, lying along my legs with his great big back on days I was just too damned depressed to crawl out from under the covers. Reassuring, protecting, comforting.

Cancer took him in our sleep when I was eighteen.

Even the day before he passed, when he was too tired from the tumors filling his lungs to bound or run, he still would roll, slowly pushing through the discomfort, for just one second of my hand rubbing his belly.

My eyes feel wet.

Dammit.

Shoving Oathbreaker into the coat, I drop to my knees beside the skinhound. He twists, bending sideways, still on his back but now able to look at me with his awful cardinal eye. He's grotesque, all exposed muscle and traceries of veins stitched together with gristle and cartilage. The muscles of his stomach are thin and stretched and, this close, I can see the fiber of them through a mostly translucent membrane that glistens wetly. I reach out slowly, waiting for him to lunge and snap his jaws shut on my throat.

His whipcord tail of vertebrae and gristle thumps against the floor.

Just like Winston used to wag his tail when I would bend to give him the belly rub.

My fingers stroke the membrane and it's slick under them and firm, neither warm nor cold. At my touch the tail goes wild, beating the tile like a drum. The skinhound cracks his jaws. His blister-pink tongue lolls out onto the floor and he begins panting.

Just like Winston.

I kneel in a supernaturally empty hospital hallway, stroking the belly of a dissected hellhound, as big, hot tears stream down my face and magick leaks out into a pool around us.

29

THE SPELL AROUND me crackles. Whatever magick isolated us in the hallway, apart from all the life and activity that has to be inside this hospital, falls in a stinging winter rain of broken spellcraft, like tiny shards of cold spearing into me all around.

Until it begins to come apart I didn't feel it at all.

And I didn't put it there.

Maybe the skinhound?

How powerful is this thing?

Sound returns to me slowly, pushing through the crumbling magick. First the low and unobtrusive Muzak of the hospital, some loungified version of a mid-nineties pop hit, starts like a wind-up phonograph, dragging in the beginning and ramping to full speed over the course of many seconds. As it locks into place I can *feel* the presence of people. They press against me like the living things they are. People in rooms breathing and talking and eating and living even with whatever illness brought them here. People walking and working, attending patients.

The spell begins to slip faster, fleeing away with each second.

We aren't going to be alone much longer.

I push myself up, the coat moving out from under my feet. That's reassuring. If the coat hadn't been alive it would have tripped me.

"C'mon, boy." I keep my voice quick and low. The skinhound rolls to his feet in an explosion of movement that is violent and graceful at the same time. He moves right to my side, head even with my hip, and follows me back to Daniel's room.

The envelope of sound around me presses closer. If anyone comes out of any room and sees the skinhound there's no telling what chaos will erupt.

My hand hits the door and it flies open.

Javier jerks short, his chest against my palm and his face twisted with surprise. Before he can say anything I push him back into the room and step in. The skinhound slips by me like a shadow.

I shut the door as Javier exclaims, "*Madre Dios!*"

I turn into the room and he's moved to the corner, hands out and a look of fear on his face. Ashtoreth stands beside Daniel's bed, arms crossed and one eyebrow ticked up in amusement.

"You just *keep* making friends, don't you, Charlie?"

"Apparently I'm charming."

She licks her lips. "You do have your charms, even hidden under that coat of yours."

The innuendo stops me cold. "Why'd you go there?"

She shrugs. "The door was open. I simply walked through."

"Don't hit on me."

"I didn't hit you."

"Goddammit, Ashtoreth."

"Which one?" She actually has the nerve to smile.

The skinhound sits beside my leg.

My hand falls automatically to his head, stroking the crease behind the nubs of cartilage that once were ears.

I push out of my mind how easy it has been to accept the weird shit I keep getting thrown.

The only way out is through.

Javier drops his hands and steps out of the corner. "I thought the coyote was bad?"

I look at him. "Things change at a moment's notice in this game, Javi. You gotta keep up and be ready for anything."

"Can you trust it?"

"She can trust it," Ashtoreth says. "That is a creature without artifice."

"What does that mean?" I ask.

She gives me a look; is it . . . wistful? Best word I can find for it. "When you have no lips, you're always smiling."

Javier looks from her to me. "Did you understand that?"

"No," I say, "but I don't have time for the enigmatic bullshit of gods, even ones who are my friends. We need to find a way to track the Man in Black."

Ashtoreth comes around the bed. "Isn't that what this is?"

"What *what* is?"

She drops to her knees in front of the skinhound. She falls with no reservation, hitting so hard I hear the *thunk* of bone on tile. Her hands move up to the skinhound's face and I pull mine back. She begins stroking the bunched groups of muscle at the back of his bone-cracking jaws.

"This *magnificent* creature is your tie to the Lord of Nightmares."

"Who?" Javier asks.

"Nyarlathotep," Ashtoreth says.

"Who is who again?"

"The Man in Black, Javi. Please keep up."

"Too many *chorra* names for one person," he mutters, his accent riding heavy on *chorra*.

My brain stumbles over her words as things fall into place. This skinhound attacked me right before the Man in Black appeared for the first time. Him saving me was the reason I felt pushed into going with him in the first place. Anytime I had doubts, shortly thereafter this skinhound would appear and I would keep on helping the Man in Black.

I was set up.

Motherfucking, conniving, bastard chaos gods.

One more thing I owe you for.

30

THE SKINHOUND IS curled up on the pull-out chair beside Daniel's bed. I think the skinhound's sleeping, but it's hard to tell when he doesn't have eyelids to close. His breathing is even and steady and matches the rhythm of the machine attached to Daniel.

It's just me and the skinhound and Daniel in the room.

Javier and Ashtoreth are wandering around outside. He promised to keep her out of trouble.

I hope it will work.

Daniel lies on the bed, not moving other than the mechanical rise and fall of his chest in time with the machine. I watch his eyelids, looking for some movement to indicate that he's dreaming, but they are perfectly smooth. The thin skin shines in the low fluorescent light, as if it has a light coating of oil on it.

His face is perfect, dark hair fallen back off it so I can study it. He's not model pretty, not even catalog pretty, but he's got strong features that are easy to follow with your eyes. Nothing to snag your vision, no sharp edges or pointy bits. Nice cheekbones and chin, eyes that aren't too far apart or too small, and if by some miracle he were to snap out of this coma you would see that they are deep emerald and luminescent with the joy of life.

I look to his mouth and I remember our first kiss. My first kiss. I feel the memory on my own lips.

And even as I smile I hate the Man in Black just a little bit more.

Soon and very soon, you black-hearted bastard. I'm coming now and this time I will end you.

Two knocks and the door to the room opens.

The skinhound is off the chair and between me and the man in nurses' scrubs who just entered as if by magick. His hackles bunch around the column of his neck and they vibrate as a growl rolls out of his vivisected chest.

The man freezes so sharply his skid-free shoes still squeak on the tile, eyes so wide that even from here I can see white completely around his irises.

I snap the fingers on my right hand and my Mark flares and I feel it jolt down the invisible connection between me and the skinhound.

I need to name the damn thing.

He turns his head to look at me over his shoulder and stops growling.

"He's a friend."

The skinhound swivels his head toward the man, then back at me. After a long second the skinhound *chuffs* through the holes he uses for nostrils, turns, and slowly climbs back into the puddle of ichor he left in the chair. He turns in a circle, nails scratching on the man-made material, before dropping back to where he was before the man entered the room. The skinhound squirms down into the cushion, settling back into place.

The man hasn't moved, wide eyes still locked on the skinhound.

"Hey, Lionel," I say softly, "it's okay. Come on in."

He steps in, eyes moving from the skinhound to me and back; they're zigging and zagging rapidly. Lionel's freaking out. He's a trauma nurse, so his freaking out is internal, not running in terror, but it's still happening inside him.

But he's here.

He points at the chair. "Um, pardon my French, Jane, but what the fuck is that?"

"That's . . . Winnie." At the name the skinhound raises his head and pants. I guess he's okay with it.

Winnie the Skinhound.

That'd make a hell of a children's book.

I speak to draw Lionel's attention back to me. "Thanks for coming in."

His eyes slide my way and focus and I see it when he just files away the weird. That nurse training must be some real shit. "I'm on shift in a few hours anyway."

"I still appreciate it."

He nods.

"I'm not going to be here much longer."

"I'm surprised you're here now," he says. "It's been weeks."

"I've been busy. Things have been weird."

His eyes go to the skinhound. "No shit, Sherlock."

Lionel is still a bit of an asshole, but I don't rise to the bait. "When I leave I'm going to be doing things that, hopefully, will fix this."

"And you want me to keep watching over John?"

I nod.

"So, this is you saying good-bye to him?"

"I plan on coming back."

"But you might not?"

"I might not."

We look at each other for a long time. Finally, he says, "You should come back or don't go."

"If I don't go, he will never wake up."

His eyes flick to the skinhound sleeping on the chair. "I don't believe in hinky shit. Not even a little. My whole family is convinced my nana's ghost lives in my mother's closet, but not me."

I shrug. "I don't believe in hinky shit either."

"You're talking about hinky shit now, aren't you?"

"The hinkiest shit you could ever imagine."

He thinks for a long moment. "Okay then."

"Okay? That was quick."

He shrugs. "Don't have much choice when the hinky shit is right in front of me. I still don't think Nana is hanging around in a closet, but maybe this Sunday I'll open the door and take a peek."

I nod, but I am tired of this walking around the conversation and the pressure of the mission in front of me is riding my back. I put my hand on Daniel's chest. His heartbeat is steady under my palm, a sign that his body is not the problem, not what is keeping him in his comatose state.

"His name is Daniel Alexander Langford. He's twenty-four years old and he was a wrestling champion in high school. That should be enough information for you to find him online and track down his parents."

Lionel blinks at me. "You really think you might not come back."

"What I have to do isn't going to be a walk in the park."

"How long do you want me to wait before using this information?"

"One week."

"I'll wait two."

I shake my head. It's generous, but if I don't make it back the magick that I did to keep Daniel here off the books might stop working.

Probably will stop working.

"One week. It won't take that long. But if I'm not back by then find his parents and let them take him home."

Lionel moves to the other side of the bed. It puts the skin-hound behind him, but he doesn't seem worried about it. Lionel really does adapt quickly. He looks down at the bed. "Daniel, huh?"

"Yes."

He nods. "I can see it. I had him pegged for a Mark in my head, but he does look like a Daniel, now that I know. Not Dan or Danny but Daniel."

"Never Dan or Danny." I'm quoting something Daniel said in our first conversation.

The door opens. Javier and Ashtoreth walk in holding armfuls of flowers and balloons. The skinhound raises his head but stays on the chair. Lionel turns. "They with you?"

"Yes."

The two of them come in and begin putting the things they carry around the room without talking. They quickly have every spare surface covered. The room seems to brighten immediately. My throat feels tight and the skin under my eyes grows warm.

I refuse to cry again.

I lean down and press my lips to Daniel's forehead.

I'm not crying; you're crying.

31

MY FINGERTIPS ARE slippery.

Winnie the skinhound is coated in something like mineral oil; it's light and odorless and absorbs quickly into my skin.

I'm not thinking about that part.

"This is going to work?"

Ashtoreth kneels across from me, Winnie lies between us. Her hands hover above Winnie's flank. Small crackles of magick jump between her and him. It looks like spatters of bacon grease, near translucent and popping quickly. Winnie doesn't move or show any sign that what she's doing is hurting him.

She doesn't answer me, just keeps with the magick hands, looking vaguely over my left shoulder.

"Well?" I prod again.

I see Javier move from the corner of my eye. "She probably needs to concentrate."

Ashtoreth doesn't say anything, but her mouth moves in a twitch of smile.

"It's not like she's afraid to talk. She does it. A lot," Javier says. "Did it the whole way to the gift shop downstairs and the whole way back."

So I shut up and wait for the whore goddess to work, but it isn't easy. This is it. I can feel it. This is the key to finally finding the Man in Black. Weeks of looking and I'm going to be able to hunt him down and get back Daniel's life force.

TO *DESTROY* THE GODDAMNED MAN IN BLACK WHO DUMPED ME INTO THIS WORLD OF ELDER GOD *SHIT.*

Whoa.

That was *more* than anger. That was raw, seething *fury.* That thought just stabbed me to my core.

Immediately I capture it and push it into a box just like I learned in therapy. I put it there and I look down on it, disconnected from it, studying it, putting it outside of my brain function so it doesn't interfere. Because I know I'm angry at Nyarlathotep, but emotions like that one cause me to do things that will only wind up hurting myself or someone I love.

Having parsed that feeling out and separating from it, I know exactly what made me react like that.

I love Daniel. Before the Man in Black put him in the coma, he said that he loved me, and I actually believe him.

But it's been weeks that he's been stuck in this hospital because I haven't been able to find Nyarlathotep. Weeks of me tracking down creatures who had any trace of the Man in Black on them. I've fought and killed them trying to find him.

I've tortured some of them.

I've done horrible, bloody things in my pursuit.

For him, for Daniel.

But Daniel is a kind soul. He's not weak, but one of the things that drew me to him, that made it possible to let him inside, was his gentle soul. Daniel is the guy next door, the friend who is always there. He's just . . . *nice,* so very nice, and so very, very normal.

Will he see me, learn the things I've done, and hate me for them?

He will know. He will sense it, smell it on me like blood I can't wash off.

And I was fucked up to start with; how fucked up am I now?

Fucked up enough that I'm kneeling on the floor beside Daniel's bed wrapped in the still-living skin of an archangel with a cursed sword and other magickal objects in its pockets petting my skinless dog while my new friend the whore goddess searches him with magick for a way to track down and kill a chaos god.

And I'm eager to do it.

Deep down in my heart of hearts, that most secret place inside me, I don't think there is a "normal" that I want to go back to.

Oh gods, I *am* fucked up.

Ashtoreth rocks back on her heels and lets out a breath forceful enough that I feel it on my face. She's been holding it awhile. "It can be done."

"Let's do it then."

Her mouth is a hard line for a long moment.

"What?" I ask.

"You should consider what we may be going into."

"Doesn't matter. I'll go to the ends of the earth to get him."

"Charlie, please." Her fingers begin pulling the hair that hangs beside her face. "I know you have dealt with the Crawling Chaos, but—"

"There you go with the 'buts' again."

"I just want you to know that you are dealing with very bloodthirsty gods. Nyarlathotep is the embodiment of chaos and destruction. He is the only begotten son of Azathoth, the Mad God, the Maelstrom of Insanity at the center of Creation."

"Jesus, laying it on a little thick, aren't you?"

She blinks at me. "You joke about this?"

I fight to keep the edge of my voice soft. "I've not only 'dealt' with the Man in Black; I've sent his Crawling Chaos ass running."

The coat around me trills at the back of my brain, not loudly, just a small, nagging singsong noise.

Yes, I couldn't have done it without you.

The coat falls silent again, satisfied.

"But—"

"Stop," I cut her off. "I don't know your history with him, but I feel like you've known him for a long time."

Her head nods slowly, down and then up.

"Do you think he has abandoned his plan to free Amazoth—"

"Azathoth." She says it quickly, like a knife between the ribs, in then out.

"Whatever, not the point, do you think he has quit on his plans and is now going to sit on a beach somewhere drinking mai tais and watching sunsets?"

She giggles. I wasn't trying to be funny. "No, I do not think that."

"Then let's dispense with all this warning crap and get down to business." I glance over my shoulder. "You still in, Javi?"

He steps forward and sits next to me.

I take that as a yes.

Winnie the skinhound nudges Javier's leg with his head. Javier reaches out, his fingers hesitating for a long moment before he lets his hand fall and begins stroking Winnie on the back of his neck. His fingers make a soft *bahh-loop!* sound, like a muffled xylophone across the exposed vertebrae.

"That's not what I thought he would feel like," Javier says.

"Yeah, me either."

Winnie's whipcord tail thumps the tile.

Ashtoreth puts her hand on Winnie and pets him with us and we share a moment of perfect peace.

We should have enjoyed it more.

32

THE COAT IS afraid.

I can feel it vibrating on my skin as it stretches around the four of us on the outside of the skinhound in the center, binding us all five together.

Javier is afraid.

With him standing to my right, our bodies pressed in a line from hip to shoulder, it rolls off him so strongly I can smell it in the back of my teeth like copper pennies in a hot pan.

Winnie is excited.

He pants, leaning against my legs like a big cat inside the cocoon of the coat.

Ashtoreth has her mouth pressed against mine.

We are not kissing.

I've had enough kissing.

But she claims this is the only chaste way for her to guide my wish ability to take us to the Man in Black. She is a goddess of love and sex. Her magick only works one way.

So her lips surround mine, which stay in a hard line. Her magick presses in and my bottom jaw goes numb, tingling from my chin to my earlobes. The front of my brain says to just open up, just let her in, it's only a kiss. My logic. The Rational.

The back of my brain, the lizard part, screams for me to fight and resist. The intuition. The Primal.

A third part of my mind dispassionately wonders why I didn't have any triggers when me and Javier did this earlier. I was hesitant, but the lizard voice in my head was quiet. Now it is full-on screaming.

Dissociation.

My head has worked this way since that night at fourteen.

I feel her tongue worm against my lips and I clench my teeth.

My hands move to push her back, landing on her arms, when the magick bursts and floods my skull, shutting down all the voices and thoughts and even concepts in a blast of raw, goddess-level power.

My entire existence goes bitter yellow, so sharp it pricks me to my marrow, and I am drowning in it, not pulled down—that would imply that I have weight and substance—no, I am completely and absolutely overwhelmed.

Washed away.

Snuffed out.

Until the coat digs its way into my mind and snags me just as I am almost swallowed up.

I grab that black tendril and pull myself back to the surface.

And there I find the world opened up to me.

It's my mindspace, the spot in my magick I use to find things. Here I feel desire like pinpricks that draw my attention. It's like a map but not like a map at all. It's mindspace. It's magick. It's not reality in a way that is normal.

Hard to describe.

I can see Javier like he's been smudged, a finger-painted version of himself spattered with water. I don't study him, letting my mind's eye slide over him before his desires can be revealed to me.

Besides, Ashtoreth is in front of me, a tower of lustful colour that pulls my mind's eye as if hooks have embedded in it.

She is a golden shape, hollow and semi-translucent. Magenta desire, chartreuse want, and cerulean need all burst inside her bleeding into one another in a firework rainbow symphony that is less beautiful and far more sinister.

Charlie, her voice skin-slips along the membrane of my thoughts, *are you aware?*

I am.

Good. I thought this might be overwhelming to you.

Her concern annoys me.

Friends worry about each other, don't they?

Her knowing my feelings annoys me more.

What do I need to do?

Look to—

The thing she says in my head is like a burst of static. It squelches and buzzes and it hurts like sizzling bacon grease running along the folds and grooves of my brain.

"What the hell was *that,* Ash?"

Sorry. Look to . . . what is your name for him? . . . Winnie.

My mind's eye shifts down, where my feet would be if I were in my own head instead of being in my own head.

Mindspace is weird.

Winnie is a hard shape. Most things in this part of my head are not static. They pulse and shimmer and shine and wink and mostly look as if they are underwater. The skinhound is the first thing I've ever Seen that has hard edges. It appears as if he has been coated in latex so black it shines blue. A hard line of bright crimson, so luminescent it is almost neon, crackles between me and him, our link, my magick, bonding us together.

Do you see it?

"What am I looking for, Ash?"

The connection to . . . Nyarlathotep.

I focus my attention, narrowing in on Winnie's representation here. I scan him with my mind's eye, rolling over his sleek shape.

I don't see . . .

Wait.

At the bottom of his left paw I find it. A tiny thread the colour of dead man's blood. It spools out into mindspace, running on for a long time. I study it closely.

It's almost nothing, the barest hint of a connection, a true loose end.

But at the other end I can feel him.

The Man in Black.

Gotcha.

I gather us up, make a wish, and shove us down the line, clinging to the thread as our guide.

33

WE TUMBLE OUT onto hard-packed earth like coins turned out of pockets.

I lie on my back and suck in oxygen, fighting away white and red spots that swarm from the corners of my closed eyes. There is no air in wish travel and that was a long trip. The longest I've ever jumped. Full of fearsome colours and malignant planets who tracked us as we passed. I don't know if wish travel is through another dimension or through outer space or something else altogether but it's so coldly alien that every moment in it causes you to feel as if you are folding in on yourself, that you are so insignificant you should cease to exist, not a suggestion of such but the truth of it irrefutable and absolute, and it makes your humanity feel as if it is a candle flame that has been snuffed by the finger of God.

Something cold and wet licks the side of my face.

I open my eyes to find the skinhound standing over

me with his head cocked sideways, looking down at me with his one egg yolk of an eye.

It takes me a few seconds' concentration to push out, "Hey, Winnie."

His teeth part and that overlong, blister pink tongue flops from his jaws, lying over the jagged line of teeth embedded in bone. I push his head away before he can lick me again.

A rustling sound to my left makes me look over. Ashtoreth is rising to her feet. She's changed. Somewhere in the trip she has shifted forms, slipped from the body she was in to a new one. Her hair is still dark as crow feathers, but now it twists and twirls around her face, gorgonesque, a nest of snakes. She's taller and definitively more . . . mature, the swells and curves of her body exaggerated against the loose silver shift her clothes have become. She is everything woman: earth mother, seductress, queen, nymph, and sorceress all at once, bathed in three miles of feminine mystique.

Her skin has become a dark lavender that gleams against the simple clothing she wears.

She is barefoot.

She is afraid.

I can see it in the tension of her supple jaw and the tightness of her eyes and in every line of her new form and it makes me pull it together.

We are not safe.

Javier.

I roll to sitting and gather my legs under me and find him curled into a fetal position in a pile of dead leaves.

He's crying, softly, to himself.

I move toward him, taking in our surroundings as I do.

We are in a clearing in a forest. Gnarled, twisted trees stretch over us, branches interlocked against the sun. The light that manages to leak through them is dim, watery, and gray like water polluted with ink. Dead leaves that rustle and move and swirl even though the air is still against my face litter the ground at my feet.

I kneel. "Javi, you okay?"

He doesn't respond, just continues weeping bitterly.

I touch him and his skin jumps under my fingers, the nerves underneath it twitching and jerking.

"Javi? What happened?"

It takes a long moment, but finally his voice comes. It's cracked and raspy, and strained. "I've never seen things so terrible."

"What did you—" Before I can finish the question the coat nudges my mind and I have—not a memory, more an impression, of Javier pulling on me frantically, tugging down the part of me that covers his face. The part of me that covers his eyes as we teleport here.

Not me. The coat. He pulled down the coat when his lungs ran short of air.

The things I spoke of that you pass through while wishing . . . if you aren't prepared . . .

"The worst part of it is that I couldn't scream, Charlie." He rolls over and looks up at me with red-rimmed rabbit eyes. "I couldn't scream at all."

I want to gather him into my arms and hold him.

Instead I say, "Good thing, Javi. You wouldn't want to draw their attention."

The skinhound growls.

Ashtoreth is there beside me.

She speaks from the corner of her mouth. "You must get up."

"Give me a second."

"They are almost here and they cannot find you on your knees."

"Javi needs—"

Her face whips down, inches from mine. Black tresses of hair spill against my cheeks, she gets so close. The fear jolts hop in her eyes and this near I can see that what looks like black is actually the darkest tone of yellow, the same colour as a solar eclipse. Her teeth are sharp and white as she bares them, hissing, "I helped you as you asked. You owe me safety. Stand and protect us as is your duty."

Flinging my arm up, I shoo her off and stand.

On my feet I can feel what she meant. Something moves toward us down the dark trail across the clearing. Something powerful.

My hand reaches into the coat.

"Do not draw your weapon. Here that is an act of war."

"I'm fine with that," I snap.

"You brought us here, Charlie. For the sake of all of us, eat your stubbornness."

I want to pull the sword. Whatever comes is moving like a high-pressure front across the ocean. Its steps vibrate my shinbones through the soles of my boots and its breath makes the leaves on the trees above shake free and fall like rain around us.

"You sure about this?" I ask her.

It is a long second before she says, "Yes."

I don't believe her.

But I stand here, unarmed, and wait.

I can draw my sword quick enough.

I can.

The air grows thick, coldly humid, and clammy. It's hard to breathe, like a wet cloth is pressed over my mouth. Despite the weak sunlight still pouring down, the shadows thicken, slithering through the woods around us until all I can see of the forest floor is the nearest trunks of the trees that soar above.

My stomach tightens, a knot inside my body, and I can't remember when the last time I ate was.

Oh yeah. At the rest stop.

Even as my breath curls into a wisp of fog in front of my face I'm sweating under my clothes and it makes me feel tacky all over like I've been painted in honey and then got dressed. The urge to shake out of the coat so I can cool off hits me strongly and I shrug my shoulders without thinking about it.

The coat screams at me.

The wail of it slices across the backs of my eyes, an ice pick through my temples, so shocking it makes me seize on the inside.

What the . . . ?

Realization drops on me like a sack of cement. I was about to take off the coat. I would have put aside its help and the items it holds inside itself. Oathbreaker. The Aqedah. Any other things I haven't discovered yet.

I'd have been not just unarmed but *dis*armed.

Now that I know it I can feel, under the cold and the dark, the softly subtle spell, like perfume on a spring day, that has been working on me. It creeps along the ground and gently laps against me. Insidious.

Sneaky, sneaky.

Reaching inside, I spark my own magick to life, pushing it through my blood, letting it course through me and burn away the influence.

My right hand glows from the inside as the Mark on my palm lights up with spellwork. Glancing down, I can see the tracery of my veins and the phalanges like shadows under the skin.

The oncoming presence stills, pausing just outside of the clearing. It stands there, in the shadows, where it cannot be seen.

The skinhound growls so low I feel it more than hear it.

"Shush, Winnie," I say. "Javi, get up."

The skinhound goes silent, standing by my hip. Javier climbs to his feet with a groan and sways over them. His arms are crossed over his stomach and his head is low, but he's standing.

I speak out the side of my mouth to Ashtoreth, watching the trail. "I thought you were taking us to the Man in Black."

"He is near."

"Where?"

"Near," she snaps. "What more do you want from me?"

I want you to put me in front of the red-handed bastard.

But I bite my tongue. She did the best she could.

Time stretches around us as we wait for the thing in the shadows to come forward. I want to glance at Ashtoreth, to get some clue as to how we should proceed, but I don't. This is my hunt. My mission.

Like she said: *I* brought them here.

Fuck it.

I take three steps forward, nudging the coat as I do. It flares out around me like batwings, sweeping a swirl of leaves behind me as I stride. Each step I drive my magick down my arm and into my Mark until it crackles and pops, dripping etheric energy in fat crimson gobbets. They fall and sizzle as they strike the dead leaves, bursting them into tiny bonfires that are snuffed out by the coat as I walk, creating a trail of smoke behind me.

Raising my hand, I shove more magick into it, making my Mark flare in the darkness and the words from my mouth roll like thunder.

"I am Charlotte Tristan Moore and I am here to claim my vengeance on the one called Nyarlathotep."

It takes a long moment for the echo of my words to fade. When it does there is a quiver in the shadows and the thing that has approached steps into the fading light where I can see it.

Oh.

34

A BLUE GIRL stands, unassuming, across from me.

Her skin is smooth, unblemished but not untarnished, as faint patches of copper green patina swirl over and around limbs and torso and head that are all the palest shade of glacial blue. Her lips and hair match, both an electrified cobalt, the hair looking as if it had been actually electrified, wisps and strands of it twisting and falling in a chaotic cascade around the narrow wedge of her face.

She is tiny.

Like a child, but with nothing childlike about her. No innocence, no vulnerability, no youth. Somehow her age sits heavy upon her, a rock on stretched linen, pulling down with weight and undeniable gravity. This one is ancient.

Dark holes sit where her eyes should be. Something glitters deep in the cavities, not the shimmery shine of something precious, but the wink and lie of bait.

Keep your fingers out of her eyes.

The thought intrudes, pushing its way in. I push it right back out.

The light seems to be falling *into* her, as if she is sucking it from the forest, leeching it into herself. She appears so delicate, but I'm sure by the feel of her she could level the trees around us if she chose.

"Who are you?" I call across the distance.

Her head tilts and I feel her blink at me although no lid shutters down and then up to disturb those wells of darkness she calls eyes.

"You ask my *name*?"

The voice is the slice of a sharp knife, so quick and clean you don't feel the cut until you are growing cold from bleeding out.

"Careful, Charlie," Ashtoreth murmurs behind me.

"Yeah," Javier says, his voice low but tight with fear. "She's creeptastic to the fullest."

I've learned that names are important in this world. They mean things, more than they mean in our world. Every being in this weird reality has multiple names and titles and they all seem important in their own way. It's why I used my full proper name, stating exactly who I am. "I want to know what I am dealing with."

She looks at me for a long heartbeat before straightening, clasping the hem of her ruffled skirt between delicate fingers, and walking toward me. Her hips swivel with each step; her footfalls stab the soft earth under my feet, leaving round divots lying behind her like breadcrumbs.

As she draws closer she begins to speak.

"I am the Fetcher. The Collector. The Gatherer."

Closer.

"I am the Hunter in the Dark."

Closer.

"The Shatterer of Bones and She Who Sucks the Marrow."

Almost.

"The Hound of Carcosa."

She stops, close enough for me to touch.

She smiles without showing teeth, thin cerulean skin pulled tight over the sparrow bones of her face and her lips stretched into strips of nothing. "You may call me Mylendor."

I let her names and titles wash over me as I stare into the black pits of her eyes, rolling them through my mind, gauging the situation.

Fetcher, Collector, Gatherer, Hunter.

Hound.

"All right, Mylie, good to meet you." I smile at her and I make a point to bare my teeth. "Now be a good doggie and take me and mine to your master."

35

THE TRAIL HAS been narrow and twisty, a rocky foot trail between brambles and thickets and sticky-sharp vines that snag and tug on the coat. It is all worked up and chattering in the back of my mind. The collar of it has ruffled across my neck like an avant-garde fashion accessory that fans around the back of my head from jaw to jaw. It clings tightly to me and I don't feel the prick of thorns, but something warm trickles onto the back of my left hand stuck in the coat's pocket and I know whatever the coat has for blood is leaking out and running down where a nasty snag has opened it up.

Of course the vegetation parts as Mylendor leads us down the trail, flowing in behind her like water, a Moses of the weeds.

I don't know where we are. If this is Earth or some other realm. I'm no botanist, don't spend a lot of time out of the city, I like walls and doors and locks and houses with places to get away if there is danger. Being out in the open like this, especially an open that is so pressed and choked with vegetation, where anything could hide close enough to touch and I wouldn't be able to see it coming, makes the panic bell ring in the back of my head where my spine meets my skull.

I don't like it. I don't like it at all.

And I don't like not knowing where I am. I have learned that even on Earth other places can exist, just steps away; one wrong turn, one pass through a door left ajar, and you can find yourself in a place people should never be. I once walked down some stairs under a sushi joint in a city I think was New York and wound up in a cave somewhere else with a massive elder god named Cthulhu in a jar.

But there's nothing to do but follow Mylendor wherever she's taking us.

The trail is so narrow that we walk in single file. I follow Mylendor, the skinhound a step behind followed by Javier and then Ashtoreth. The skinhound refused to be farther away and I trust Ashtoreth to defend herself far better than Javier could, so she brings up the rear. I don't like being so closed in, so I concentrate on the soft blue and green glow of the skin on the back of Mylendor's neck and put one foot in front of the other when all I want to do is pull out Oathbreaker and use it to hack our way free.

The air has gone cloying, thick with the stifling perfume of vegetation, not rot as much as decay, cellulose breaking down, the nose-ruffling odor of chlorophyll exposed to humid air. It's fetid. Dank. Musty.

Familiar.

In my fourth-grade Earth Science class, Miss Kimbrough brought in a botanist who lived and studied in the Okefenokee Swamp. She showed us pictures of alligators as long as cars and flowers with such colour they made my young eyes hurt with their beauty. She also brought with her a mason jar of swamp water. It sat on her table full of displays, caught in a ray of sunlight that made the glass gleam like diamonds but wasn't strong enough to cut through the water itself, water that remained murky and thick with effulgence of dead vegetation and some other alchemy my young mind could not comprehend. The light entered the jar on one side and exited the other as a dark green shadow that stretched out onto the desk as the botanist continued to talk. Finally, she lifted the jar and unscrewed the lid with a muffled *pop*. For a moment she stood there smiling as we all waited.

I was sure something alive would stir inside that murky water and crawl out, slithering wetly across the back of her hand to flop on the table, some salamander of ancient design that would stand in a puddle of its own liquid and stare at me with red cast eyes like drops of blood turned to pearls.

I held my breath in anticipation.

I was the last to discover what did come out of that jar.

Tommy Hanson was the first to react, pinching his nose and exclaiming loudly. His example was quickly taken up, round-robin, in a chorus through the classroom.

One girl, I just remember her with bramble-thick blond hair and freckles across her nose, began to retch and choke as if she were sick.

I looked around, letting free my captive breath, and, on inhaling, discovered what my classmates already knew.

That small jar of swamp water had tainted every bit of oxygen in the room with the same fecund green odor that tries to take my breath right now.

It's a relief when the trail ends and we break free to the open field.

Oxygen, cool and damp, rolls against us as we step into the knee-high grass. Mylendor continues forward, but I stop. Ashtoreth, Javier, and the skinhound stop as well, Winnie moving up and leaning into me, his blind socket against my thigh.

Javier whistles softly. "You don't see that every day."

In the center of the field is a house.

But not just a house, a house that looks like it has been taken apart and then reassembled with the corpses of a dozen other houses. It's a jumble of weirdly shaped rooms and roof lines, samples from a dozen styles of architecture and time spans all smashed together without rhyme or reason. Here there's a patch of a pueblo-style adobe that blends into the sleek glass and steel of a modern art deco house that slides into a stucco ranch. There are chimneys that jut into the tree line beside doors on upper stories that have no stairs or porches. The very front of it looks as if it has been plucked from the movie *Gone with the Wind* and placed here in this untouched clearing. Looming from the ground, it gleams in white. The front has a set of wide steps that lead to a terraced porch with mighty columns rising three stories to its roof. The windows are aglow with buttery light that spills through them without tinting the soft, pale gleam of the building itself.

As we watch, the front doors open inward as if being swallowed by the house and more golden light fills the space without colouring the porch or the columns.

Mylendor turns her head just enough that I can see her profile, even as she keeps walking, and says: "Come now, Charlotte Tristan Moore; do not fall behind; my master awaits."

Her voice sounds like she's mocking me.

She may be.

I feel like I'm being torn in two. I want to follow her. No, I want to run her down and grab her by the hair and drag her to that house and see what kind of thing waits inside.

I want to do that.

I do not want to take Javier inside there. Or Ashtoreth.

Or even Winnie.

This feels like a trap.

I fell for a trap all those years ago because I didn't see it. I didn't see Tyler Woods maneuvering me away from the party and into his room, where the other three waited. I didn't see it and I paid for it.

I still pay for it.

Now I look for traps.

Sometimes I see them almost everywhere.

I reach over, past Javier, and lightly touch Ashtoreth on the arm. Her skin is damp. "Can you get them out of here?"

She shakes her head. "Without you the forest would consume us."

Javier pushes against my arm. "I'm in this."

The skinhound whines and gives a short, sharp bark as he trots forward a few steps and then looks back at me.

"I can wish us back," I say.

"We are too far away. If you take that much from Javier he will be in the same condition as your Daniel."

My Daniel.

The reason I'm doing all of this.

Is he?

Shut up.

"I'm fine," Javier says.

He says it forcefully and I take a close look at him. He's standing straight, but his eyes are set in deep smudges of dark, like he's pulled three days with no sleep, and there's a tic yammering like a hummingbird's heartbeat that has set up in the corner of his upper lip. He needs rest and replenishment, neither of which I have here. My eyes slide past him to Ashtoreth, who slowly shakes her head side to side as if to confirm my analysis of him and his condition.

I just stopped in to see what condition my condition was in.

The only way out is through.

"Stay close," I growl.

And, one foot in front of the other, we follow the creepy Hound of Carcosa to the creepy patchwork house in the middle of the creepy fucking forest.

36

THE INSIDE OF the house is no less creepy than the outside.

Crossing the threshold puts us inside a foyer straight out of a Gothic cathedral, complete with a fountain in the center that bubbles something too thick to be water, even though it's clear. The syrupish fluid rolls over the marble scallops, dripping and drizzling into the wide, oval pool of the fountain well. I glance over and things swim in the fluid, long, thin things that look like eels except they have vestigial arms and legs that trail beside them uselessly. One of them turns and wriggles upward, grape-sized head breaking the surface with a low *gah-loop!* sound. It shakes its too-human face to clear it of the viscous liquid, micromouth moving as it spits globs of the stuff free until I can hear its voice like the subsonic mewling of an injured bat. The weight of the fluid drags at it until it slips back under the surface and begins swimming in circles again.

Ashtoreth bumps me with her arm.

Mylendor is farther ahead, not looking back.

Moving away from the grotesquery of the fountain, I follow her, my boots squeaking slightly on the mosaic tile of the foyer. We step onto a thick shag carpet from the seventies as we walk into a hallway that only goes for perhaps nine yards before breaking into stairs and landings that lead off to nowhere.

Javier's voice comes up from behind me. "This place is freaky deaky."

"It will get deakier," Ashtoreth says gravely. "Welcome to the ways of my kind."

Winnie makes a noise in his chest. It sounds like skinhound for "shut up."

We pass by candelabras flickering next to incandescent bulbs that barely glow, the glass of them looking hand blown, thick in some areas, soap-bubble thin in others, the squiggly wire of them glowing dull orange like coals in an abandoned brazier on a forgotten altar somewhere, and I get the impression they are old, far older than I.

We pass by a flickering sign for a beer brand that boasts clear mountain water as an ingredient.

My boots sound off on wood planks as the flooring under them transitions again.

A window set in a brick wall opens on my left, making me spin and jerk away. The coat feels my tension and reacts like a cat, flaring around me in a swirl of inky darkness.

Winnie's claws *click-clack* on the wood as he lunges in front of me, skinless hackles raised.

The window has a wooden sill with a flowerpot. Gingham curtains hang on the inside of it, parted just enough that I can see inside is a narrow room that holds an antique billiards table without enough room for anyone to actually play the game, even though the balls are racked and ready. The side walls touch the edge of the table, the back wall farther away and blank as a piece of paper.

There is no door I can see.

There is also no one who could have opened the window.

Fuck this crazy-quilt house. Everything is such a mix and match that it's setting every nerve I have on edge.

Mylendor chuckles ahead of me.

It makes me want to smash in the back of her head.

I start walking.

Something is off. Not just the crazy building we are in. Not just the dealing with otherworldly beings.

Something's off in me.

I look at it as we draw near a pair of doors at the end of this branch of the hallway. They are ancient timbers of dense wood going petrified, bound with iron I can smell in the back of my sinuses as we draw closer and closer. They belong on a castle of some proto-Norse warlord in some timeflung version of history.

But what is wrong with me?

This entire situation has me on edge, wound tight as if I've been laced into myself. I'm not aware, I'm *hyper*-aware, to the point of paranoia, my body reacting to my mind. Now that I've noticed it, I can feel how close my thoughts are to tumbling into panic, falling into the pure white noise of chaos where I can't think, can't plan, can't do anything but react.

Panic is an animal state, the wild mewling of a newborn mammal with its fur still slick to its body and just enough foresight to know that it is nothing more and nothing less than meat for the eating.

Scratching from the inside, scrabbling along the seams and the joints of my mind, working to wiggle even the tip of a talon between the folds and grooves of my brain, panic tries to get at me.

I panic and I lose control.

Sensei Laura's voice pours into my head. *Lose control, lose yourself, lose your battle. Panic equals destruction at the hands of your enemy.*

I stop walking.

Everyone around me stops.

"Charlie, you okay?" Javier asks.

Close my eyes. Shut out the world around me. Go inside. Fall. Breathe in through the nose, out through the mouth. Connect my tongue to the roof of my mouth to make a circuit for my ki, my life energy. Pull my thoughts into a small ball and wind them together. Control. I breathe.

In through the nose.

The stillness of a peaceful lake.

Out through the mouth.

The solidness of a stone.

In through the nose.

I am the mountain.

Out through the mouth.

I am the wind.

In through the nose.

I am water.

Out through the mouth.

I open my eyes.

Everything feels slightly fuzzy, dissociated and separate from me, as if I'm looking at everything through a slight barrier. I'm back inside myself.

I am Charlotte Tristan Moore, Wielder of Oathbreaker, Coat-wearer of Iniquity, Hunter of Nyarlathotep, Bringer of Justice to the Gods Themselves.

I am ready.

Mylendor chuckles again. "I certainly hope so, *mon ami*." Her hands grasp the iron rings bolted to the ancient wood that serve as handles and she begins to pull them apart.

"For you enter into the court of the King in Yellow."

37

Ashtoreth's voice is harsh and throaty, like she's being strangled. "Oh Jesus, not him. Not the King in Yellow."

I turn to her, not believing my ears. "Did you just invoke Jesus? Like *Jesus* Jesus?"

"Shut up, Charlie," she hisses. "This is bad; this is really, truly terrible."

"*You* just invoked our Lord and Savior; I get that it's serious."

Her eyes are wide, white showing all around the dark irises. The blood has drained from her face and her skin has gone paler and pasty. "Your sarcasm will not serve you here."

Mylendor smiles and, even though it looks perfectly pleasant, it's feral and *feels* like the corners of her mouth stretch too far back and reveal too many teeth. "Little Ishtar, do not be so concerned. The King in Yellow may very well find her . . . amusing."

"That is my fear," Ashtoreth snaps. "And do not call me by that name."

Mylendor's smile disappears. "I do not call things. I fetch them, take them in my teeth, and carry them where I want them to be."

"Where your master wants them, you mean."

"The difference is the same." Mylendor shrugs. "Ishtar is the softest name I have for you. Would you rather I use one of the other names you held here in court?"

"You've been here before?" Javier asks before I can.

Ashtoreth looks between me and Javier, off in the distance, not meeting anyone's eyes. "I have been subject under the Yellow Sign. It was long ago." Her eyes flutter shut and she shudders, just slightly. "The court moves, in time and space. I wasn't sure this is where we would end up until just a moment ago." She shudders. "I hoped against hope that Mylendor had changed masters."

"Never," Mylendor hisses.

I ignore her, still facing Ashtoreth. "A little warning would have been nice."

Her eyes are now sad and slightly shimmery along the bottom edges. "You would not have heeded it. You are on a mission."

That is true.

"If I'd known it was going to be this dangerous I would have sent you back." I mean it.

"I am with you." Her mouth is a hard line, but I can still see that glimmer deep in her eyes, that haunted shine that flits behind them when you've gone through something so traumatic it marks you forever.

Forever.

I guess that would mean something more to an immortal love goddess than it does to me. To me, things *feel* like forever; to her, they actually *are* forever.

I recognize the look; this place, this setting, this thing we are about to do, is bringing back memories of something that left a tattoo on her mind; it has scarred her psyche and she has been changed by it. I recognize that look because if I stare in the mirror too long I see it in my own eyes.

Something here hurt her in a way that will haunt her.

Forever.

I turn to Mylendor. "From now on, you address her as Ashtoreth or not at all. She is my friend and under my protection."

"If you say so." Mylendor sniffs in dismissal.

Not good enough.

I step closer. "Mark my words, if you or anyone inside this place offers her harm or even insult you *will* answer to me."

Mylendor smiles her feral smile. "Bold words, *mon ami,* bold words indeed. The King in Yellow will truly find you entertaining. It should be a lovely evening of fun and frolic." She turns and walks inside as if expecting us to follow. The doorway is full of shadow and she appears to fade with each step.

Ashtoreth reaches out and touches my chest. The coat rustles around me. Her hand is wide on my sternum, thumb resting under my breast, but it isn't even slightly sexual or possessive. "Thank you, Charlie. No one has ever claimed me . . . like that." Between the words *me* and *like* the haunted glimmer flares bright and her lower lip curves down with sadness. "When you cannot keep your word I will forgive you offering me up."

Before I can say anything she turns and steps past me.

The Mark on my right hand begins to burn and a prayer I don't believe in, that I can keep her safe, passes through my mind.

38

THE DARKNESS AROUND us begins to dissolve against some feeble, fetid, dull glow that lacks the clarity and sharpness to be called light. It is simply not darkness. The floor under my feet switches to cobblestones so tightly packed together they are smooth and seamless. The skinhound's nails *click* and *clack* on them as we follow the path. We are not in a room that I can discern; whatever the borders of this place are, they are not close enough for me to see, and I have the feeling that if I were to try to walk toward them they would run from me, ever out of sight.

It looks like we are in a room that looms far out of sight, like a hangar or some similar place, but it feels like we could be outside.

The air is slightly crisp over the back of my throat and tastes of October, All Hallows' Eve and Samhain and Día de los Muertos, that Thin Time betwixt equinox and solstice when the world is all witchery and full of pagan potential.

I loved Halloween as a kid.

Trick or treating, wearing costumes, sticky stomach from too much candy, the Headless Horseman, and ghost stories before bed. Loved it. The entire thing.

Tyler Woods's party was a Halloween party.

One more thing stolen from that night.

Goddammit.

And since the Man in Black walked through my door and dragged me into this world of weird gods and monster shit I don't think I'll ever enjoy Halloween again.

Something pulls at my eye as we walk after Mylendor, and Javier says, "What was that?"

I turn and find that the not darkness is moving, shapes forming as things begin closing behind and beside us.

The skinhound makes a noise like water being strained through garbage.

I stop and everyone stops around me, close this time. I don't reach for the sword in the coat even though I want to.

The shapes keep shuffling closer until I see they are hunched humans, each of them wearing a tattered dun-coloured coat that wraps tightly around their frames, sleeves to waists across their chests, long, flat ribbons of fabric pulled taut between their legs and spun around their thighs and torsos.

Straitjackets. They are all wearing a weird version of a straitjacket.

They shamble close enough that I can now make out faces. The same dull-eyed, institutionalized look carries through one and all. The same wet oatmeal tone to their skin regardless of race, the same ribbons of drug-thickened spittle hanging off their chins, the same slack-eyed stare that makes their bottom eyelids roll and hang forward as if wires pull on them. I can smell the waft of Thorazine in their sweat and the concerted *whoof* of their halcyon breath.

My mind tries to throw itself back, to spin me into a full-blown body memory of my time in Beacon Hill.

After that night, after the trial, after life was supposed to go back to normal, things got dark. I lost my way inside myself for a bit. I was destructive and angry, ignoring my therapist's treatment, lashing out. My parents didn't know what to do, so they sent me to Beacon Hill.

It worked.

Not because that place did anything to help me. That place was hell on earth. They ascribed to a regimen of heavy psychotropic drugs and harsh "aversion" therapy to cure deeply disturbed patients. I watched as the other patients either spent their time in a walking coma, so chemically straitjacketed that they weren't even human, or were "corrected" for negative behaviors with shock therapy, water therapy (the military calls it waterboarding), and even receiving blows from the rubber batons carried by every sadistic orderly.

It worked because my three days in there showed me how bad things could get if I didn't start taking my pain seriously and work on my therapy. My parents came to check on me before Beacon Hill said they could and saw the fear in my eyes. They pulled me out immediately and took me home.

I was supposed to get my first shot of some kind of drug cocktail that night because I had refused to take the pills they gave me. The director had sat with me that morning in her beige office with the dying ficus in the corner that smelled like a drying corpse and explained that if I didn't swallow the pills she had in her hand then that night the orderlies on duty would strap me to a gurney and they would inject me with a dose that would ensure that I could "relax and begin to heal."

I thank God that I wasn't left, strapped to a gurney, drugged out of my mind, and in the care of those sadists.

I should return there, when all of this is over, if I live through this thing, and teach that staff the same lesson Tyler and his crew learned not long ago when I accidentally wished me and Daniel with them and my magick and the hate in my heart killed them all.

The thought runs up my spine in a dark thrill, galloping fast and hard into my brain. It feels so good. Delicious. I immediately shut it down, clamping on to it and shunting it to its own corner of my mind lest my power kick in and I find myself in the cafeteria of Beacon Hill.

"They aren't the dangerous things here."

Ashtoreth's voice pulls me out. I have to blink, but I'm back in the moment. We start walking again, the shambling mass stumbling in behind us. The cobblestones take us to a courtyard that opens to feel weirdly enclosed even though I cannot see a roof or walls.

But I do see the throne.

39

THE THRONE LOOMS into the soft not dark, taller than me by three times and leaning precariously. At first I think it's made of crystal, each facet cut from the next with a weird gleam on its edge that has no light source to create it, but on closer look it appears to be plastic. Hard and shiny and segmented, layers and layers of it against one another.

High at the crest of it sits a man.

Man might be presumptuous; it *feels* masculine but doesn't feel human in any way, like Ashtoreth feels feminine. He slumps in the seat of the throne covered in what looks to be a blanket or a poncho in some material the colour of wolf urine. We stop far enough back that I can look up at him without causing pain in my neck.

"Who is that?" I whisper to Ashtoreth.

Mylendor appears, stepping from the darkness, the movement everything like a cat. "You stand before the Yellow Sign of Hastur the Rambler, he who drinks men's minds and sups their souls. Show your respect at your own peril."

"Never mind." I don't whisper this time.

At the calling of his name the man leans forward, shifting. The entire throne sways toward us, bending with a wide hiss of stridulation that sounds like a ragged bow drawn across a broken fiddle, catgut snagging on snarled wire and splintered wood. His legs splay out and his feet touch the earth in front of me and I see that the throne is made of layer upon layer of translucent rounded triangles segmented by seams of fibrous material the colour of the cotton in a smoked cigarette filter. They rustle and rub, drawing my eye to them, past the man-thing attached to them, to their cicada shape and form as they rise and fold and rise and fold and rise and fold into themselves in some infinite origami of reduction. Wings. They are wings, insectual and diaphanous, a wasp, a hornet, a stinging winging thing that can inject venom into you over and over and over again until your bloodstream fills with the stuff and it begins to dissolve your muscles and makes your tendons pull and contract as they stiffen and draw in a rictus that snaps the very bones they are attached to.

The wings fold away, disappearing from sight as his poncho shifts over them. Not a throne at all. A perch provided by his own wings.

Once they slip-slide out of sight I can look up at his face. It's an upside-down triangle, chin to a point and eyes wide across a short snout of a nose that squats over a mouth too full and sensuous to make sense on that face. His hair falls over in a sweep of darkness with an undefined edge, as if his head simply fades away into the not darkness. He doesn't blink for a long moment as he looks down at me.

And then he does.

And his eyes change from softly unfocused to razor-sharp and honed into the meat of me and I feel his gaze on the pulse in my throat.

I do not step back from him.

It takes everything I have not to.

The coat draws tight around me, hardening against my skin, becoming like armor as its voice burbles in the bottom layer of my brain.

He turns his face toward Mylendor, but his eyes stay on mine. "What sweetmeats have you brought to my table this time, faithful hound?"

His voice is so normal it's a shock. He sounds like any man with a mid-timbre voice that would speak to you about the weather.

"I came here under my own power and authority. No one brought me." I know how these things work, so I answer before Mylendor can and I put an edge on my voice like a machete. "And I am no fucking sweetmeat."

"You travel with bits and bites, my darling; I made an assumption." His eyes slide to Ashtoreth and even through the coat I feel her go tense, every part of her vibrating as her head drops and her eyes fall to the floor.

Winnie the hound *click-clacks* to her, a long growl shaking his frame. Long, thin ropes of the ichor that coats him hang and sway from his vivisected chest.

The Yellow Man's upper lip curls back. "I will staple your skin back on, *Conmortavich.*" He spits the last word. Is it a name, an insult? "You are no protection for her. Not here."

Mylendor slides sideways, to the Yellow Man's left side, covering his flank. Her skull has gone flatter, the bones shifting, giving a leonine cast to her features. Her body sinks, center of gravity lowering.

The air vibrates with her own low growl.

The coat sings frantically up into my brain.

The choir of patients around us take up a round-robin moaning that slithers between us, moving in and out, a long python of undulation.

Ashtoreth shakes, fine trembles running under her skin like

many-legged things chasing one another. The panic screams off her and she might collapse in on herself.

Javier stands close to her, face nearly blank, and I don't know if he's scared or in shock or oblivious to what's about to explode around him.

When you're outnumbered act quickly and decisively.

I decide what I'm doing and the coat agrees, so I shake magick into the Mark on my palm and make my move.

40

THE COAT GOES soft and supple around me, flaring out like a dragon wing as I push off on my left foot. It stretches out and up, forming a wall of solid darkness between my people and the bad guys. Mylendor rolls away, her feline body twisting and curling in on itself as she does. The King in Yellow jolts back, poncho flapping, snapping at the chill air as he tries to get away.

I'm on him before he moves a full step.

My left hand curls in the fabric of his poncho, fingers digging for purchase. The cloth is thick, like sailcloth, but brittle, dry-rotted, and my fingers tear through it. They sink in and hit something hard and smooth.

His wings, flits across my mind as I scrabble around for something to grip, to grab, to hold on to, so my strike has as much power behind it as I can muster.

My right hand is a magenta comet, surrounded by a nimbus of etheric energy that crackles and sparks. Master Ken's gruff voice jabs in my mind, the words from his lessons long ago just as harsh and unforgiving as he was a teacher.

All your strength every strike! Hit to destroy your opponent.

I punch through my body, using my hips for torque, driving with my whole torso and not just my shoulder. My fist is a stone from a catapult, a runaway train, a nuclear warhead of magick and physical potential.

I drive it into the King in Yellow's chest.

And everything explodes.

The backlash of magick slams into me and it feels like a cannonball trying to take my head off my shoulders. My feet leave me and I drop, slapping onto the cobblestones. My skin goes raw from magickburn, scoured by the very energy I unleashed, and my eyes turn all black deep and pure as if they've been plucked from their sockets. I lie, pinned to the ground by the weight of my own body, the coat limp around me and moaning in my head.

As my vision clears I see the King in Yellow.

Standing over me.

And smiling.

41

"Mayhaps that was a mistake," he says.

I push myself up to sitting and slide back from the looming King in Yellow as the coat coils itself back toward me. Once I get a few feet between me and him I glance around.

He and I are the only two conscious.

Javier and Ashtoreth lie next to each other, his arm across her, neither of them within five feet of where they stood when my spellpunch went off. Winnie the skinhound has his back against Ashtoreth's side and I have to look hard to see his splay-ribbed sides moving. Mylendor is sprawled against a mound of unconscious mental patients, arms and legs tangled in their straps and jackets. The coat is silent and still, full of drag like I went swimming in the damn thing and it's waterlogged.

My feet almost stick to the coat as I climb to them. As I fight to not trip and face-plant into the cobblestones I become acutely aware of how much it normally helps me move. It hums along my skin ever so slightly and I am sure it's not dead, but I don't know just how badly hurt it may be. The silence in my head is cavernous, pressing against the inside of my cranium, and it's hard to think my own thoughts without the constant gurgle of noise from the coat for them to skim over. Since I woke wearing it my brain has had a stream of alien song running in the background and without it I am left feeling that my synapses are misfiring and the chemical connections that form my thoughts are loosely fitted and could slip their sockets at any second.

Wake up soon. I push out to the coat.

The King in Yellow moves and my attention is brought back to him.

The thoughts in my brain tighten, squeezing together as I realize that with the coat non-responsive (unconscious?) I can't get to the weapons inside it.

No Oathbreaker.

No Aqedah.

No soul gem.

I am weaponless.

HELPLESS?

No.

I full-stop *refuse* that thought. Push it away with violence.

My bone marrow turns to ice water as the King in Yellow stares at me. His left eye drifts to the outside, disturbing for its laziness, as if it is unconcerned with the thing before it and has wandered away to see something else to hold its attention.

Thoughts are straying.

Moving around untethered in my skull.

I shake my head to clear it.

He takes my movement another way and the eyebrow over his lazy eye slides up. "Oh, you think otherwise?"

"What?" I ask. So clever.

"You shake your head at my claim that your assault was a mistake." He takes a long step in my direction. "You say that you committed no error?"

Act as if. Hold your ground. Be a wolverine.

"Of course I do." I don't know what else to say.

"You threw your magick at me to no effect." He chuckles and in it I hear an echo of the stridulation of his wings. "Seems a mistake to me."

I catch a loose thread in my unraveled thoughts and grab on to it. "No effect?" I raise my own eyebrow and sweep my hand over the people lying around us and the words come to me. "You attempted to harm those under my protection. Now they slumber peacefully as I guard them and your intentions toward them have disappeared."

He straightens at this. For a long moment he seems to contemplate what I said. "My intentions toward them *have* changed, moppet." His smile creeps back into place. "But you should worry that my intentions toward you have changed also."

"Do I look worried?" I push my eyebrow up higher, going for cocky, and try to make my face take on a sardonic, reckless casualness that doesn't truly feel successful.

That lazy eye of his rolls in its socket, near-black iris moving my way until it lands in my direction and rocks to and fro like a roulette ball before settling in its socket and staring at me.

Always bet on red.

The stare has weight to it and lies heavy against my skin, saturates my flesh to the bone, as if I've been underwater for weeks and then dug out all swollen and full and sloshy. It soaks me and my lungs tighten as if the bottoms of them are sodden cardboard, unable to pull molecules of oxygen from the breath I drag into them.

I break the look and begin studying my nails.

They are ragged, chewed to the quick; the cuticles one and all have tissue-thin strips of skin waving in the air over narrow furrows of painful pink flesh.

He isn't used to humans, not sane ones, (yeah, like I'm sane); I can feel it. He seems to hold court with the gibbering lunatics.

Like the song goes: *I've always been crazy, but it's kept me from going insane.*

"Mayhaps you are a fool. Mayhaps you are ignorant of who I am."

I don't tear the little bit of skin off my index finger cuticle even though I desperately want to. The habit rides me hard. One therapist suggested that biting my nails was a very passive form of self-harm for me.

I told her there was nothing passive about it.

But I'm not removing a bit of my skin in this place with this monster here before me.

I put my hands in the pockets of the coat. They feel just like regular pockets on a regular leather coat, but as my fingertips caress the smooth lining of them a small murmur begins at the base of my brain. A glance tells me that Winnie the skinhound is beginning to move a bit.

I just need a little more time.

I fake a yawn. "Let's see, Hayster the rumbly, King of Yaller, master of a toothless hound, and a sign of some kind."

Mylendor lifts her head but doesn't stand. "I can show how toothless I am, meatstick."

The King in Yellow moves his hand in her direction, silencing her. "You missed the most important title I have. The reason I may allow you to live another day."

I don't respond. I just wait for it.

He leans in, looming over me again.

"I am the Concubine of Shupnikkurat, Paramour of the Black Goat of the Woods with a Thousand Young, mated to Baphomet Midnightress."

I don't know what that means but the words strike chords deep inside, engendering a bad feeling about them, so I say: "I don't know what that means."

He blinks at me and the action makes his lazy eye drift. "Have you never been in love?"

Daniel comes to the forefront of my mind. I put the thought of him away, protecting it. I don't know if the King in Yellow can read minds, but too many things can. "I don't know what that means to *me*." I shrug and the coat shifts on me. It's lighter than a second ago; it's waking up, coming to. "Right now it doesn't concern me at all."

"Oh, but it does. It is the basis for the agreement between us."

"I have agreed to nothing."

"Did you darken my court with no purpose?" He sniffs and his voice rises to a higher pitch; it gives his words more of a buzz, like he has a throat full of honeybees. "I scoff at this notion."

Before I can speak something changes. Like a shift in the ozone when a storm is approaching or the flash of clarity that you get right before the drunk driver smashes into your car, and my spine is suddenly painted in ice water. I shiver inside the coat and it tightens around me and its voice begins to babble in my head and the dread inside me builds until I am not surprised when it happens.

It feels inevitable, inexorable, unstoppable.

"She has come for me."

I turn.

With a sinister chuckle he rises, separating from the not darkness like a splinter pushing through flesh. I've never seen him without the coat that hangs around me. He's an ebon blade: long, slender, and sharp. Made for puncturing lungs through rib cages. He's sleek and beautiful and oh so, so deadly.

A ghost.

A god.

A guru.

In an impeccable suit with his red right hand.

The godsdamned, motherfucking Man in Black.

42

"HELLO, ACOLYTE."

The Crawling Chaos stands before me and tilts his head as he addresses me. He smiles and his lips stay closed, but I know that behind them is a mouth full of shark teeth, jagged and serrated, designed to cut meat from bone. His jawline is still clean and jackal long, his nose still bladed and sitting between hooded, heavy-lidded eyes. Hair now hangs over his brow in a careless shag of ebony that falls to blend at the shoulders of his suit. The white of his collar is pure but doesn't gleam, doesn't reflect off his dusky skin. He is tall and thin and of an enviable height.

I feel small.

Over the burbling voice of the coat is a rising tide of white noise. It's panic, unadulterated fear spilling across my thoughts, drowning them.

The Man in Black raises his hand, his red right hand, and lightly strokes his chin with skinless fingers. I stare at it and my eyes go fuzzy, but my mind blazes with the memory of it, at the raw fibers of the muscles, the flat strings of tendons laid over them in a lattice of pull and relax, tension and release. The veins and nerves all pulse over the thin red membrane that covers the whole thing, clinging to the palm and pads of the fingers, lying over the knuckles and dorsum, rolling over the wrist joint and disappearing under the linen cuff of his shirt. I see it all in my mind's eye and I remember all the times he touched me with that hand, cool, dry, slick, and the crackle of elder god hoodoo.

The coat tightens across my chest and something solid digs into my ribs below my breast.

The white noise gets louder.

The coat squeezes again, harder, the solid thing presses hard enough to bruise, and it slices through the panic and I know what it is.

The hilt of Oathbreaker.

The coat is telling me the cursed blade is available from its fathomless depths, only a split-second's reach inside.

The coat is all the way back and I am armed.

I take in air with that thought and it clears my head like wind on a foggy morning.

"I'm not your Acolyte."

This smile parts his lips just slightly and I see a gleam of white. "Then what are you to me, Charlotte Tristan Moore?"

I push aside all the implications of that question. I am not going to get into a war of words with the Lord of Nightmares. "Your executioner."

The King in Yellow shakes his head, stepping forward. His arms are crossed, hands inside the ragged sleeves of his poncho. He looks even more insectish than before, like a praying mantis or some other form of locust. "He is owned, Little Godslayer; you may not claim him."

I stare at him. "What?"

"He is mine, caught and tagged." His arm slides out of the sleeve and he extends it toward me. On a wrist that is all skin and bone hangs a gold bracelet made of fine chain and tiny charms in the form of multi-legged creatures. It shines as if lit from within, giving the metal the illusion of being liquid. The King in Yellow tilts his head toward Nyarlathotep, who raises his red right hand and gives it a shake. A matching bracelet tumbles down and hangs against the raw crimson flesh and nicotine-coloured tendons. I watch the two of them clench their hands in sync, matching bracelets flaring brighter and tinkling like mad fairies.

As I watch the Man in Black I see the ring.

On the third finger of that red right hand sits a silver ring with a stone the colour of spring grass.

The colour of my love's eyes.

The colour of Daniel's eyes.

It slips, rattling between the knuckles. It is the essence of Daniel, his soul or something much like it. The Man in Black took it the last time I saw him. It's the reason Daniel has been in a coma for these last months. I need that ring to fix Daniel, to restore him.

The King in Yellow snaps his fingers, drawing my eyes from the ring. "If you want to kill him you must earn him."

I smile and drop my hand into the pocket of the coat. My fingers find what I am reaching for and the Mark on my palm begins to tingle as they close on it and draw it out.

In my hand is a long knife with a heavy spine and a wedge-shaped iron blade set in a plain wood handle, both of them stained with ancient blood. The Aqedah. The Knife of Abraham. I raise it between me and the King in Yellow.

"What do I have to do to just take a finger?"

"I do not offer him piecemeal, Little Godslayer."

The Man in Black clears his throat. "You should not offer me at all."

The King in Yellow turns. "You stumbled into my court seeking asylum, wounded at her hand and leaking yourself upon my flagstones. You knelt before my throne and sought the Yellow Sign to protect you from her. You brought her into my court."

"I did no such thing. She has made it clear I have no control over her."

"Your actions before your service to me sparked her desire to find you. Your fortunes have fallen since you attempted to make her yours. I have need of her service and she has designs on your life, or at the least your finger. I own you, Lord of Nightmares. I am Hastur, the Rambling God, and I will strike whatever bargain I wish with you as the collateral."

He turns back to me.

"He's slumming it now?" I ask.

The King in Yellow just looks at me and I see he doesn't understand the question.

I try again. "He's busted, he's broke, and he works for you now?"

I get a nod of the head as assent.

I laugh and it feels good. "Oh, how the mighty have fallen! The big, bad Crawling Chaos groveling at the feet of another."

"I do not grovel," the Man in Black says.

"You will if you become mine." I see Mylendor climb to her feet. She's still shaky from the backlash of my magick.

Or she's faking it really well.

My people are stirring but still out.

The coat rustles around me.

The King in Yellow glances down at the Aqedah.

"I do not allow weapons in my court."

The words of Mr. Han, the Kali instructor who visited my dojo and taught knife fighting, come out of my mouth. "It's not a weapon, it's a tool."

"It has killed," he says. "You have killed with it."

I look past him at the Man in Black. "Did he hear that from you?"

The chaos god shrugs. He actually manages to look sheepish.

My mouth tastes sour. "It was first used to carve wood. It's a tool."

"Put it away and we can talk."

I shake the knife in my hand. "This knife cut through him"—I point at the Man in Black with the blade—"as if he were butter. You said it hurt him so bad you were able to capture him."

"I spoke true."

"I bet it would do the same to just about any god I stuck it in."

"It would." The King in Yellow nods. "But not as quick as she can tear out your companion's throat."

A purring growl starts to the left and I look to find Ashtoreth wrapped in Mylendor's arms. The Hound's hand has transformed into something multi-jointed and curved with talons that shine like volcanic glass dug into the fallen love goddess's neck. Ashtoreth's eyes are wide and she mouths something that looks like, *I'm sorry*.

The motion brings tiny trickles of blood that seep from where points of talons meet thin skin.

I drop the ancient knife back into the coat's pocket even though I don't want to. "Let's negotiate."

The King in Yellow smiles. "As you wish."

I hate you.

He waves his hand back toward the Man in Black. "Take care of the *Conmortavich*. He will be pesky otherwise."

The Man in Black turns and steps toward the skinhound, his red right hand hanging limply above the striated tissue stretched over the rack that is the skinhound's rib cage. It crackles with etheric energy, descending slowly.

Then it stops in midair.

The King in Yellow grunts.

The Crawling Chaos folds himself, dropping to a crouch beside the nightmare hellhound that he set after me to drive me into his plans. He hovers on his haunches, head cocked as raw-knuckled fingers twitch and quiver, each minuscule movement causing magick to spatter from them.

His voice drifts over. "What have you done here, Charlotte Tristan Moore?"

Ashtoreth speaks and the effort brings fresh blood around Mylendor's claws. "She tamed your pet, Seed of Azathoth."

"Do not name my father again, tiny goddess. It will not go well with you."

Ashtoreth goes silent.

The Man in Black looks at me. "What have you made my slave into?"

I don't know what he is talking about, so I shrug and smile and hope it's cryptic enough to keep him off-balance.

"Is it?" The King in Yellow speaks over his shoulder.

The Man in Black shakes his head. "It cannot be. She has changed him, but not to that extent."

"Then cage him and let us be about our negotiation."

The Man in Black shifts, twisting on the balls of his feet. His shoulders move and his elbows go in and out of sight around the wide taper of his back.

I take a step forward.

Ashtoreth hisses and it sounds like a dozen cobras, making me look at her. Her eyes are wide and screaming for me to stay put.

When I turn back the Man in Black is rising. Winnie the skinhound is awake and twisting, his face wrapped in an iron cage muzzle that lets his jaws part just enough for his blister pink tongue to loll out and hang. He shakes his head and drops it to the cobblestones, banging sparks from the rusted iron as he beats and beats and beats his face against the rock, trying to dislodge the cage.

The coat flaps and flutters around me, agitated.

The adrenaline burns along my blood, chasing magick that runs from my sternum to the Mark inscribed in my hand. I let my eyes shift over to See for a mere second and pick up the thread that connects me to the skinhound and I push magick down it. It runs to the hellhound like quicksilver, swirling through him until it hits the cage and reverberates back to me along the connection.

The mask feels like just a mask, just bits of iron forged and hinged together but nothing more.

Nothing ensorcerelled.

Nothing spelljinxed.

Nothing conjured or consecrated.

Just metal, plain and pure.

Deep behind my breastbone a shard of ice crystallizes. It crackle-spreads through my chest, settling around my heart like hoarfrost in deep Norse winter. I hold that cold, my mind a still lake, placid surface not betraying anything that might dwell in the dark, murky depths.

When I speak I let the winter into my voice.

"Stop."

The word goes straight to the skinhound. He arches his knobbed spine as if I have shocked him and drops to his belly. The iron muzzle scrapes on the ground as he rolls his one baleful yellow eye in my direction. The long pink tongue, now dry and covered with dirt, slurps up between the jagged teeth in his exposed jawbone and he whimpers.

I keep eye contact with him. The coat trills and I lock it out of my mind for a moment. "Does it hurt?"

The skinhound raises a crescent-clawed paw and swipes at the cage. The black nails of it *ching* off the rusted metal. He shakes his head with a snort that blows wet across the metal that rests against his teeth, turning orange iron oxide into the colour of dried blood.

"Endure it for a moment then. It will not last, I promise."

The skinhound whimpers but lays his caged head on skinless paws.

The coat shifts, settling back in place.

Lifting my arms in what could be interpreted as a signal of peaceable intent, I look the King in Yellow dead in his lazy eye and say, "Tell me what I have to do to kill that red-handed bastard and don't you dare jerk me around."

43

HASTUR MOTIONS WITH his hand and from the edges of the not dark I see movement. His followers struggle to their knees, movements hampered by their straitjackets. They begin crawling away from us, knees thumping dully on the cobblestones, making a rhythmic beat below the thrashing sound the thick canvas of their jackets makes rubbing against itself like a barrel of snakes being shaken. The noise crawls along my nerves and I have to fight to not let that pull my shoulders up around my neck.

To distract myself from the sensation I point at Mylendor. "Let her go."

Mylendor snarls at me and her tongue is forked and flickering among needle-thin and curling cat teeth. Her eyes slide over to the King in Yellow and he nods. Her mouth moves and that tongue flicks up, swiping across Ashtoreth's jawline.

"Just as I remember you tasting," she hisses.

Ashtoreth doesn't move, doesn't react, frozen in place save for a tightening around her eyes.

It makes my jaw clench so hard my teeth hurt to see it.

In my ice-cold heart I put Mylendor on the list.

Her claw moves from Ashtoreth's throat and she stands, all liquid grace and catlike, and when she reaches her full height her hand has returned to normal. She raises it to her mouth and the tips of her slender fingers are still tinged red from the pinpricks of Ashtoreth's blood. She moves beside the King in Yellow and leans against him, offering her hand up to him.

He leans his head down.

"Just so you know"—I let my voice take a hard edge—"*this* is jerking me around."

His eyes roll up at me as his head stops moving.

"Get on with it or I am going to lose my patience."

He straightens. "What is patience to someone like me? I have all of eternity."

"No, you don't. You're on my timetable. Tell me what you want for Nyarlathotep or me and mine are gone."

"Yours?"

"Yes."

Where is Javier?

The Man in Black chuckles.

The King in Yellow chuckles.

As if my thought calls him, he steps through the crawling mass of straitjacketed people. He looks the same but shaky, like he's cold. He moves over by Ashtoreth and the skinhound. She puts her arms around him and he leans against her.

Questions roil in my head like storm clouds on the open water.

"Do you want the task you have to perform, my little Heracles?" Hastur asks. "After all, you did arrive under the Yellow Sign with a purpose."

"I'm not your little anything." I push my questions aside. "Say it."

He coughs into his hand and a small cloud of black dots, like tiny fruit flies, swarm from his mouth. "Have you ever been in love?"

"None of your business."

The Man in Black says, "That is the reason she has come."

I put my hand up toward him. "Stay out of this."

"You are bargaining for me; I will not sit idly by." He waggles the fingers on his red right hand and the spring grass stone glimmers. "Her paramour's essence."

The King in Yellow nods sagely. "So you *have* been in love. I assumed as much."

"What does that mean?" The words growl out between my teeth.

He indicates with a loose-wristed hand that motions toward my face, the gold bracelet that holds the Man in Black captive shimmies around Hastur's wrist, and for a second I am tempted to grab it. "You wear the bauble of Ishtar." He indicates the collar around my throat. He mentions it and I suddenly feel it around my throat, heavier than it was a moment ago.

"Ashtoreth," I correct.

"The same." He smiles. "So you know the *touch* of a love goddess. As I do."

The emphasis he makes on the word *touch* causes little insect wriggles along the inside of my skull.

My mouth opens to speak, but Ashtoreth beats me to it.

"The Great She of May-Eve is not a love goddess."

The mask slips on the King in Yellow and I see a glimpse of the thing behind it, so cruelly beautiful it hurts the backs of my eyes. My vision is still in the non-magick range, so it is a real thing, not my perception. She upset him with that sentence and he slipped, just a tiny bit.

I file it away.

"That is true." He doesn't look at Ashtoreth, keeping his eyes on me. "She is no *mere* sex goddess to be passed around the court to anyone who wants to take their piece . . ."

He's not watching Ashtoreth, but I am. His words are causing her to flinch, like blows that can't be seen.

I know how much words can hurt.

Asked for it.

Deserved it.

Probably a whore.

I heard them all after the newspapers ran the story of what happened to me.

Magick boils in my throat as I speak. It coats every word and I can feel it like venom spilling down my chin. *"Don't say another goddamn word about her."*

He stops talking.

"I am done with this." I jab my finger toward him, coat ruffling around me. "You gods and your games."

I'll kill every last one of you.

He doesn't smile, but I can feel that he wants to.

"We are eternal. Games are the only thing that we have," the Man in Black says.

"And stories," the King in Yellow says.

"Yes, the stories," the Man in Black agrees.

The King in Yellow smiles. "Then I will tell the story of Us."

"You two?"

"Not Nyarlathotep and me, that would be a boring old tale of captivity and slavery and one being bent to the will of the other. You will hear instead the story of the greatest love your universe has ever been privy to."

I shake my head. *"You* may be eternal, but I don't have time for this."

He acts as if I said nothing and continues on. "I saw her across a smoky universe . . ."

"Here we go again," Mylendor hisses, licking her fingers like a cat licks its paws after a kill.

And once he begins I can't tell him to stop.

44

———

"I SAW HER across a smoky universe, wild and wanton and free in her creative destruction. I found her squatting over the carcass of a planet she had hunted down, arms deep inside it scooping out the meat of it. Streams of sweetly rancid mother's milk ran from her teats and down her sides to mingle with the honeyjuice that slickened her thighs and her aroma, oh, the *scent* of her, filled me with a desire I had never known!

"Desire to rage across time itself in search of one spare second.

"Desire to comb an infinite beachhead for one perfect grain of sand.

"Desire to taste every corpuscle ever circulated to find the one perfect strand of genetic substance.

"I moved to her; to get the attention of such a creature as her, I arrayed myself in all my finery, and went to her. She looked up as I approached and in that second she measured me, shook me, pressed me down, and found me wanting her. She sniffed once and her mouths smiled small, sly smiles that made thunder in my belly.

"She gave a little, mocking laugh, turned, and ran.

"The chase was on.

"I stumbled and tripped through the universe, always one step behind, just missing her around an asteroid belt, or almost touching her and then having her slip through some small crack to another layer of subspace. I chased her through singing stars and cold dead voids. I chased her through the colour out of time. I chased her through fire and ice and nothingness and vast stretches of memory and the psychic collectives of countless planets. I tore apart worlds to locate her scent when I slipped the trail.

"I thought I'd lost her a dozen times and every time I was on the edge of giving up I would hear her teasing laugh and I would know that she still wanted me to chase her, to hunt her down. That the game wasn't just in my head.

"Finally, on plains of psychotromic emotions from a race of long-dead people I caught her.

"I latched on to her and we tumbled, lying amid all the hate and fear that had resulted in worldwide genocide on a planet on the other side of the universe.

"There we made love.

"And as I entered her I understood: I realized that she was vast and so much more than I. This was Shupnikkurat, the goddess of life and fertility; from her was everything born and from her will everything give birth. Every moment of creation in every galaxy she was there. In every piece of artwork, in every dream, in every story ever told, every curse spoken, every time anything new was made there was her touch. Her mark is upon the very fabric of existence and I was hers, completely.

"That night, lying there, cooling in our sated lust, fluids drying under a dying red sun, we had our first child.

"It was a mewling little thing, all long limbs and spine and teeth. It kicked in its amniotic fluid between us, nipping at our fingers as we stroked it and knew the fulfillment of parentage. This was *ours,* the combining of *us* brought forth into existence, and as it found its feet we pledged ourselves to each other, for all of eternity and beyond.

"And now someone has taken her, trapped her on your plane of existence, and I need you to bring my love back to me."

45

MY EYES BURN and are wet, tears tickling as they hang from my jawline.

I don't wipe them. I leave them there. I'm crying. Fuck it. I do that.

I lost all my shame over crying long ago and far away.

The King in Yellow keeps his head bowed, shoulders rounded so that his urine-coloured robe juts off them with protuberances that may or may not be from his wings. It looks like a sack of sticks and quivers in the low light.

Mylendor has turned her back to us, curling her spine so much she looks like a torso balanced on its end.

Ashtoreth and Javier weep in each other's arms, Javier's body jerking as if someone is pulling the organs from his chest.

Even Winnie the skinhound has his caged head turned sheepishly into his own shoulder.

The Man in Black is smiling.

It throws ice water on the sorrow inside me.

This feeling, all this cotton candy sticky love and adoration and longing, isn't real. It's a trick; I've been magicked by an elder god, one who, at best, doesn't care about my species and, at worst, wants to actively destroy it. I contemplate the emotion in Hastur's story of intergalactic elder god lust and I know in my heart of hearts he isn't indifferent to humanity like he claims.

I speak and my words are breaking glass in a silent room; everyone looks up.

"Why do you need me to rescue her?"

He looks up at me. "She has been captured by your kind."

"Send him." I point.

Hastur glances at the Man in Black.

"You've got him on a string; let him go get your . . . what would you call her?"

"Queen, wife, lover, mistress, helpmeet."

"No, her name."

"Shupnikkurat, Shub Niggurath, Black Goat with—"

I throw up my hand. "I get it. *Shubbie* will do."

"I would not suggest you call her such."

"Point is, you've got the Crawling fucking Chaos at your beck and call. I'm just a regular little human. Seems like he could swoop in and save your . . ."—the word is distasteful applied to them even as I say it—"wife."

"He cannot perform this task."

I pull the thread. "Then he is worthless. Give him to me."

Hastur shakes his head with a small, rueful smile. "Not so easy, Twice-Marked."

Twice-Marked?

I don't dwell. I move on. "Why not?"

"She is held by your kind. If they can capture her in all her glory then they can take even him."

"Sounds like my kind of people."

"They are humans."

"Could be worse; they could be *gods*." Spit leaves my mouth on that last word.

"Your kind are a mold, a *stain,* on the universe. You seek and destroy anything including yourselves. You are nothing—you are less than that; you are a *nith*."

"And yet one of my kind has captured your queen and you are asking this . . . what did you call me and mine? . . . this *stain* for help."

"It does gall me."

I look him in his lazy, drifting eye and point at the Man in Black. "Do you know what *he* does to your kind?"

"He is my thrall; it does not matter."

I see it when it happens. The Man in Black stiffens at Hastur's words, shoulders widening, and he doesn't move, but he seems to lengthen, stretching and growing darker until all I can see is the whites of his eyes and the gleam of the low light along the edge of his red right hand and I file it away. There is something there I can possibly use.

"He comes with me."

The Man in Black turns to me sharply and Hastur simply looks amused. "Why would I send him?"

I shrug. "You said he is yours to command. He's a cannon. I've dealt with humans who capture your kind. I might need a cannon."

Hastur and Nyarlathotep both study me with their heads tilted. "You will attack the moment you are away from my sight," Hastur says.

"I wouldn't think of it."

It was absolutely my plan.

"No need to think of it." He smiles his nicotine-tinged smile. "I've already thought of it."

It's too confident. Too cocky.

Oh no.

Light flares to my left, two dozen or more feet away. It's a torch, coming to life. It's stuck in the crook of one of the asylum patients' arm, wedged in where the straitjacket wraps him tight. It's too close to his face and I can see the skin blistering and turning red as meat on a grill.

He doesn't seem to notice.

Instead he steps back and another torch held by another lunatic flares to life. I watch as this happens a dozen times in as many seconds until there is a line of torches held too close by mental patients. The air is full of the smell of pitch and burning human hair. When they begin to circle around I see what they are walling in with human flesh and fire.

In the center of a ring of fire held in the arms of lunatics is Daniel on his hospital bed.

46

———

"You son of a bitch."

Hastur smiles.

Shit. Fuck. Shitfuck. I'd had Daniel safe, hidden away for months now. How did they find him?

I push the thought away. *Right here, right now. Deal with this. How and why doesn't matter.*

All that matters is Daniel.

My feet move without me directing them, speed-walking along the outlined path toward him. Once I'm by his side I find him as I left him just a few hours ago, except somehow he seems smaller, more vulnerable out here amid the crazies, instead of in a nice, safe hospital. The machines are not there with him; a sheaf of loose cords and wires hangs from under the bed-sheet where they were not brought. I touch his chest and he breathes evenly.

My hand moves to his cheek and I find the skin to be soft and some part of me that wasn't there before (I hope it wasn't there before. God, please don't let this have always been a part of me) thinks that if I pushed hard enough I could sink my fingers through his skin and into the meat of his face.

I pull back.

Fuck, what is wrong with me?

Daniel's face turns, following my fingers as they pull away.

My heart clenches, a fist nestled betwixt the sponge of my lungs.

His bottom lip trembles.

Quivers.

The thin skin is dry and even that movement makes it crack in a series of small red lines.

His mouth parts and from his throat comes the sound of a voice unused for weeks in a throat dry and abraded by a feeding tube. It's a rasp, a hasp, a choke.

But it's crystal clear in my ears.

"Charlie."

Everything turns blurry as my heart convulses and my face goes hot at the sound of my name on his lips.

I want to answer, the desire of it sits in my mouth like curdled milk, clotty and solid behind my teeth, but my throat has closed.

Or it's plugged from below by my heart being in it.

That's a metaphor.

Daniel's eyelids flutter.

"Char-lie."

I sob, but no sound escapes me; nothing betrays me there to his closed eyes save the anxious rustling of the coat around me.

I touch his arm.

His eyelids crack open, fluttering like pinned butterflies, delicate and spastic, threatening to tear themselves apart. His eyes underneath are all sclerae, white as fish bellies in the night, rolled back like the eyes of a hung man.

A gleam of emerald in the dark across from him snags my eye like a barb.

"Daniel," I breathe.

He shivers, microspasms running underneath his skin.

Emerald and crimson gleam beyond him, reading black in my peripheral where they meet.

Daniel bucks on the bed.

The Man in Black steps from the darkness as if someone has cut him from it.

And Daniel screams.

47

THE SCREAM IS long and brittle, the end of a howl.

It climbs into my ears and slices its way into my brain.

The Man in Black steps closer as the sound squeezes, pulling thin as Daniel's lungs empty of oxygen. It dwindles, spiraling into a thread that breaks, and still Daniel stays arched, face going dark with the effort to keep on screaming, jaw knotted, veins cut in bas-relief, tendons corded and vibrating as if they will snap and furl up into their sheaths leaving him with nothing to keep his throat from collapsing inward from the weight of itself.

Panic clings to me, its arms wrapped around my chest and hanging, a monkey on my back, a millstone about my neck. My magick kicks in the white-noise adrenaline rush and jolts down my arm, scorching its way across Daniel's skin.

He collapses, sucking in air as if he were drowning.

The Man in Black chuckles.

My hand plunges inside the coat.

I pull the Aqedah from the icy depths of the pocket as he flicks his red right hand toward Daniel. A spark of verdant magick kicks off the stone on the ring that sits on his finger, falling like an ember onto Daniel's lips.

I lunge with the Aqedah, but the Man in Black is too fast, already snaked back beyond my reach. I step to chase him around Daniel's bed when I hear Daniel's voice.

It stops me where I stand.

He's speaking, barely above a whisper.

It's complete gibberish.

Nonsense words, syllables strung together that sound as if they are from another language altogether, all harsh and guttural, animal sounds, and curse words all tumble from his mouth.

Then the asylum patients who surround us begin speaking the same gibberish.

The exact same.

Word for word, sound for sound, all the grunts and clicks and hisses in unison like some kind of choir of ill children linked by madness.

The Man in Black's voice crawls over it all.

"This close and the ring that holds his essence gives him a tiny sliver of himself. Imagine what it could do were you to win it from my hand."

"I'll cut it from your hand. I'll take the finger it's on," I snarl. "Hell, I'll hack off the whole fucking limb."

The shimmering sound of chitin on chitin slithers around me and from somewhere behind me comes the voice of the King in Yellow. "No, you will not. If you do you forfeit the soul of your paramour and I will create him anew as one of my torchbearers." He steps into my sight, dun-coloured poncho fluttering even though there is no breeze, and I wonder for a moment if it's alive like the coat.

The coat trills in my skull.

I don't know if that was a yes or a no and I don't care.

The King in Yellow's smile spreads wide, the teeth sharp and feral but the colour of old nicotine-tarnished Sheetrock. "The offer is simple. Go rescue my love and I will return yours. Refuse and I enslave him."

Off to the side, Nyarlathotep smiles his shark-toothed smile.

Weeks ago, the Man in Black tried to take all of Daniel's life force out of revenge. I stopped the Man in Black before he could drain it all; that's why Daniel lay here on the hospital bed.

The coat trills in my head again and this time I do understand.

Yes, you helped.

What the Man in Black took before we stopped him was enough to put Daniel in a coma he's been in until now, awake but not back. I know that given the chance, the Man in Black will finish the job out of spite.

Or do worse.

I cast around for some option, some way I can get Daniel and get free.

And come up empty.

I'm in some other elder god place, nowhere to run to, nowhere to hide.

Shit and fuck. Shitfuck.

I need an idea.

Anything.

"Do you accept my offer?"

"He still comes with me," I blurt out, pointing at the Man in Black. "I'm not leaving him out of my sight with Daniel around."

Hastur considers this. "Very well."

"Ashtoreth comes with me as well."

"Why?"

"To help watch him."

He considers this. "I will allow it."

"I want that cage off my skinhound. He and Javier are going to stay here and watch over Daniel." I'm not looking at Javier, but I can see him moving from foot to foot. He's not going to want to be left behind.

Tough shit.

Hastur looks at the Man in Black. "Skinhound?"

Nyarlathotep shrugs.

"He has no skin," Hastur says.

"I did not name him as such," the Man in Black says.

Hastur turns back to me. "He has no skin."

"It's just the name for him in my head," I say.

"You humans name things in such ridiculous ways."

"You're one to talk, Ramblin' John Hastur, Yellow King of the Great Frontier, or whatever you're titling yourself."

"I did not name myself."

"Who did?"

"Excuse me?" Jaundiced eyelids flutter at me like epileptic butterflies pinned to a board, still alive, still feeling pain.

The tension ratchets up in the air between us. "*Who* named you?"

"I, I . . ." He looks around. "I do not know. I have always been Hastur of the Yellow Sign."

"Always?" I press. His lack of surety has my nose open. There is something here. Names mean so much to these beings that him not knowing where his came from might be a sign of weakness. Might be nothing, but I will take any advantage I can get. "Surely even the gods themselves have a beginning. Who first called you that?"

He looks at the Man in Black. "Who first spoke? Do you remember?"

"I was named by my father."

"Add a hoth?" I ask.

"*Az*athoth." The Man in Black's voice is strained, tight around the words.

"Oh yeah, the crazy one. How is your pops?" I smile; I can't help it. He doesn't answer but his red right hand clenches by his side. To Hastur I say, "So, his daddy give you your name too?"

Hastur's hands flutter over his yellow poncho, rippling the tatters of it like a wayward breeze. His lazy eye keeps sliding back and forth in its socket and his upper lip trembles.

"Some say the Primal Chaos is the progenitor of everything," the Man in Black offers.

"Shamazatron is the Primal Chaos?"

"The Primal Chaos is one name for my father. Unlike *shamazatron*, which is not a word in any language."

"And you're the Crawling Chaos?"

"Yes."

"The Primal Chaos and the Crawling Chaos?"

He tilts his head in confirmation.

"Obvious much?" I sneer. It feels good on my mouth to do it.

"Azathoth is the fountain from which this universe poured forth. The first and he shall be the last." The Man in Black's voice is tightly drawn again, crossing itself.

He's really sensitive about his daddy.

I file the information away to use later.

"Enough," the King in Yellow says. He speaks softly, almost as if he isn't speaking to us at all. "None of this completes the task. Free my mate and I return the essence of yours."

"How do I find her? If they hid her from you they will have her hid from me."

The Man in Black chuckles. "Why, Former-Acolyte, that is the question indeed."

"Surely you have something of hers. I can do a full bloodhound gang if you have a token of hers, some fetish that belongs to her."

"I thought you would never ask."

Jaundiced knuckles rasp as they slip under the ragged poncho and dig around. Muffled under the dry-rotted cloth comes a chiming ring, the same sound made when you run a finger around the rim of a wineglass, a drawn-out, rubberized squeak of flesh around furled and fluted stemware.

Watching him root around inside his torso sets my nerves on

edge and that fucking noise drives them to jangling. The coat rustles around my legs and I know the noise is causing it actual pain because it echoes in the vertebrae at the top of my spine like misplaced acupuncture, a psychic loop of aching feedback.

The long, thin arm of the King in Yellow slides farther in until his forearm is completely inside and his biceps is pressed against his side. The shoulder joint separates, stretching and jutting under the poncho as his eyes, even the lazy one, drift to look over my head, fixated on some middle distance of concentration.

He grunts and shudders and his arm snaps between the elbow and shoulder.

It just breaks like a stalk of celery with a crunching pop and the bone inside forms a rough hinge under the skin and it slides ever farther into the depths. If it hurts he doesn't show it past his initial grunt.

The back of my head goes all hot and prickly.

Is it dimmer in here?

After a long moment when the world around me pulses he straightens and draws his arm out. A shake and the broken bone clicks back together with a grinding noise that makes my jaw ache. He extends it and unfurls his fingers.

Resting on the palm of his bony hand, swaying ever so slightly on the uneven surface, is a jar of smoke.

48

THE JAR PULLS my mind back in memory, back in time to Meemaw Moore and her peach preserves. Every summer we would drive up and visit and she would insist that we take back a case of them. She would spend her time picking the peaches from the trees planted long ago by her husband before he'd passed and then doing whatever alchemy transformed them from ripe fruit to pungent chunks of preserves. Dad would always take them home, always insist that we open them and eat them on toast, but the flavor was sad, as if her sorrow of being left to grow old without his father had tainted the fruit, spoiling it like milk on a warm day. We never finished the first jar of any we took home and they would sit in the pantry, inducing guilt in all of us as we reached past them to choose the simple grape or strawberry jam that came from the supermarket and didn't taste like fruit as much as a chemical equivalent but was always free of sadness and recrimination. My mother would quietly throw away the rest of them just before we would go visit again, leaving the space there on the shelf to fill again when we returned with more small jars of sour, psychically tinged fruit.

When Meemaw Moore passed on, the last of her preserves stayed in the pantry.

Last time I visited, they were still there, behind the creamed corn and the kidney beans, covered in a light dusting of time, only displaced by the accidental brushing of a knuckle that reached too far to pluck whatever sat in front of them.

The King in Yellow makes a sticky buzz noise in the back of his throat, and I'm back.

It's a simple mason jar, fat curved glass with a cheap metal lid that screws on, a lid pocked with rust, spotted with the texture of oxidization against the dully smooth tin. The smoke inside it curls and rolls against the glass as if there was something inside the jar, something obscured by the smoke like fog will obscure that stranger walking beside a river on a chill morning, something inside moving and shifting, displacing the smoke with its presence.

Something I can't see.

Is it invisible?

Is the smoke *itself* moving, somehow sentient, somehow malevolent?

Hey, life is nothing but weird shit now; that isn't the leap it would have been a few weeks ago.

"This is the only portion of her we have been able to find." The King in Yellow holds it out to me.

I don't want to take it. I know I have to, but the thing fills me with dread that sits in the pit of my stomach.

I reach out, wrap my fingers around the lid, and pull the jar off his palm.

It's like picking up a cannonball.

The weight of it jerks in my grip and I fumble it. I try to grab it with my other hand too, to catch it. I didn't expect it to have mass, smoke should be weightless, but this is solid, dense, like a jar of lead. The glass is slick on my fingertips and I get no traction and the damn thing spins out of my hands and crashes to the ground.

The sound of glass on cobblestone is a shrill scream that runs across my tightened jawline.

Glittering shards spray out, peppering the coat that has swooshed across my legs, protecting them. The shards embed in the inky surface of it like shrapnel, jutting out like sharp bits of glitter that could slice flesh as easily as a thought.

Ashtoreth gasps.

Mylendor growls.

The Man in Black chuckles.

The skinhound whines.

Javier crosses himself.

The King in Yellow doesn't move.

And I bite back the *Sorry* that tries to leap from my throat.

The smoke roils around on itself and then begins to rise, expanding larger than it should, not dissipating like it should either, sinuously climbing toward my face like a cobra at the end of a flute. I watch the smoke and I know that when it gets high enough it will crawl into my lungs.

It's just smoke.

It's just smoke.

It's just smoke.

The mantra barely keeps the staticky fuzz of anxiety at bay in the back of my skull.

"Free my skinhound," I command as the smoke crosses my waistline.

The King in Yellow nods at something behind me. When the Man in Black snaps the raw fingers of his red right hand I feel it across the skin of my brow. The cage mask clanks open and the skinhound shakes his head violently, tossing the damned thing away into the gloom that lies past us.

The smoke is at my chest.

I make my words a command, backed by the crackle of the magick in my veins. "You and Javier guard Daniel. Stay with him until I return, and repel anyone or anything that tries to harm him."

"Charlie, I—"

"Shut the fuck up, Javier."

He stops talking.

The smoke is at my throat.

"You wanted to come along. This is the price. Guard him until I return."

"You're going to make it back?" His voice is tight, full of doubt.

"I won't abandon you here." *Please let me not abandon him here.*

"Promise?"

"No matter what it takes."

The smoke brushes my chin like oily fingers.

It is cold on my lips as it rushes into my mouth and slithers to my lungs like a snake burrowing after warm-blooded prey.

49

THE SMOKE ROLLS down my esophagus, coating the sides of it like cold mineral oil, clinging as it does, and splashes into my lungs in clots of congestion, and I can't breathe because I am drowning.

My chest is solid, thick with congealed smoke and no room for precious oxygen, so heavy, too heavy to expand and draw in breath. My diaphragm pulls, a rubber seal holding too much pressure, and all I can think is that it wasn't designed to do this, to be this, to perform under this circumstance, and the world turns dark behind my eyes in a red wet throb and this is what it feels like to drown in a bog, to be sucked under the thick swamp and smothered and drowned and suffocated by things too thick to truly be water anymore, a substance that fills more than just water ever could, some primordial soup that we all came from and now tries to bond back with the flesh of me and turn me into itself and I will be no more *I*, simply more *it*.

It's beyond panic, beyond fear, too solid to be anything but inevitable.

The magick in me flares, boiling the viscosity of it away, clearing my lungs and my brain in a harsh scrub like bleached sunlight killing a mold.

I suck in air and as my hearing returns I realize Ashtoreth is gasping like I am.

The torc around my throat tingles, almost buzzing against my skin. It came from her, the thing that makes my magick able to move me through space and take others with me. She gifted it to me, at the order of the Man in Black, in a dilapidated, abandoned motel room when we first met. It ties me to her.

"You okay?" I ask her.

She nods, wiping her eyes with the backs of her hands, and they smear black streaks across her temples. I didn't know she was wearing mascara. Her face has changed since the last time I looked at her. It has the same crow black hair, but now it bounces in sweeping curls around a squarish jaw. Her features are painted copper and blunt, all the delicacy of her younger version wiped away. It is a face of someone who has seen her loved ones go off to war and now lives with the sure knowledge they will never return. A face of sorrow. Her eyes remind me of Meemaw Moore.

And, suddenly, I don't want to take her with me. I don't know where we are going, my magick does, and I have to keep pushing it back, holding it at bay so I can think about her and this and how I don't want to do this *with* her or *to* her. Wherever we go is not going to be easy; it won't be a simple thing to walk in, pick up the elder goddess mate of the King in Yellow, and skip back with her. I know too well that getting involved with these things always ends in blood and pain and things too thick to be washed off easily. This is going to hurt, in one way or the other, and I want to spare Ashtoreth any more hurt if I can.

"You don't have a choice."

Her words jar me.

The protest begins to form and I open my mouth.

She cuts me off.

"You have to take me or leave me here, and please, *please,* do not leave me here." Her eyes are wide, unblinking, imploring me as the desperation pours out of them.

Mylendor moves closer. "She can leave you behind, little Ishtar. We will gladly care for you while they are away."

I step between Ashtoreth and the Hound of Carcosa. "Back the fuck off, Fido."

Mylendor growls.

I growl in return and my magick is already up and provoked; it climbs my back like a scorpion's tail wanting to strike.

The King in Yellow speaks softly. "Heel."

Mylendor draws upright and shakes herself. She turns and slinks to his side.

"Enough," he says. "Do as we agreed."

The magick boils in my blood, filling all my ability to perceive, and I am done with all of this. Enough time has been wasted, enough energy has been expended, and I have to bring this to an end. I barely think the thought and the coat obeys, unfurling in streamers from me, wrapping both Ashtoreth and Nyarlathotep in ribbons of itself, binding them to me.

I let the magick inside me loose and the flavor of the smoke fills my mind, sweeping up from my tongue and the insides of my nostrils all bacony-charred flesh and dried wood and charcoal and something sweet and acidic and spicy that coats the inside of my mouth and won't wash away no matter how much I swallow.

I don't fucking care where we are going, I just let go and ride the magick away from this goddamned place-that-isn't-a-place and these goddamned gods.

50

I HIT THE ground knees first, and my stomach tries to crawl its way out of my throat.

Dammit, without Javier, or someone else, to be the battery my magick powered us here with my own life force to fuel it.

I swallow hard to keep the acid out of my mouth.

I'm on my knees.

There is grass under me and the night air is sticky and wet.

I shove back and stand, too fast, try to step quick and right myself, but my heel catches the edge of the coat. It pulls out from under my foot and the motion skews me sideways. I am falling and all I can do is brace for the impact.

Something clamps on my arm, halting my momentum and holding me still enough to untangle my feet.

Ashtoreth's hand holds me.

I pull free, careful to not jerk away, because I'm thankful she kept me upright.

I smile at her in gratitude and she turns her eyes away.

The Man in Black's voice is a sneer when it comes. "You should have allowed her to fall, Mother of Prostitutes."

"I will not do that." Her voice is steady but small.

"Will you not?" His hands cut through the air in front of him like drunken fish in a barrel of whiskey. "Do you not eventually let everyone fall? Is that not the definition of a whore's promise, goddess of them or not? Surely you do not think your divinity is more than your nature."

Ashtoreth doesn't reply.

I try to speak in her defense, but the sick threatens to come out if I do, pushing against the back of my tongue where it connects to my throat at the esophagus, and so I breathe through my nose with my teeth clenched and growl because I can't do more yet.

The Man in Black ignores me and stares her down, eyes dripping with dark wanton sensuality, smoldering in their sockets like hot coals. "Ah, Mystery, you are so transparent!" he cries as he sways around her, near capering, the black suit he wears hugging his frame like a second skin.

The coat flutters around me, agitated.

The Man in Black claps, fat droplets of magenta magick spattering off the red right hand, squeezed out by the impact, striking the ground in a rattle like teeth in a tin can. He leans close and his lips pull back as if by wires, exposing triple rows of jagged shark teeth in a smile made of homicide. His voice comes harsh, the rasp of file on steel. "Now why, little harlot, are you acting as if you are not going to put out when we both know that is all you are here for?"

Ashtoreth flinches with every syllable.

Goddamn *enough*.

I swallow my sick.

Two strides and I'm there. I crunch down and keep moving and ram my shoulder into his chest, swinging my elbows up on contact to drive them deep into his ribs. It's a body check learned in Greco-Roman class and it uses all my mass against his torso, the goal to drive your opponent away and off their center of gravity.

Nyarlathotep folds like a dirty towel.

My arm hits nothing but the cloth of his shirt and it feels like a stretched canvas, something pulled tight over a gap, a nothing.

He stumbles away and I watch closely; I can't believe I moved him so easily.

He stops, hunched over, red right hand pressed deep against his side. It glows a harsh yellow, the colour of mustard left to dry in the sun, the etheric energy highlighting the raw red flesh of his hand in sunset colours.

His wound.

The King in Yellow said that the wound I gave him with the Aqedah hadn't healed. I didn't realize it was so severe.

Inside me that thing that lives in my belly, that dark entity that slithers in my guts and makes me want to burn the world one shitheel at a time like a trail of struck match heads all charred and curled and sulfur stained, that thing rolls in a happy way and begins a slow climb up to my brain. If it gets there I don't know what I will become.

But I don't try to fight it back down.

Its voice is mine as I say, "Leave her alone. I've had enough of you and yours cutting at her with your implications and snide remarks."

The Man in Black eyes me sideways, hunched around the red right hand pressed to his chest. Under the spoiled butter halo of the magick from his hand is a seeping black that wicks through the fabric of his shirt in an ever-widening stain. His hand moves away, fingers sweeping down to indicate the wound.

"I see in your eyes you think this a weakness."

"Isn't it?" I smirk. "It helped nearly knock you on your ass just now."

He straightens. "Mewling human. You do not know weakness. Even with this"—his hand pulls away from the dark spot on his shirt and it begins to fade as I watch—"I am greater than you can even conceive. My will is resolute and my eye keen."

"Your eye isn't as keen as my knife."

"The knife you stole from me."

"Won from you."

"I think not."

"Ask for it back then."

"You will not return it to me."

"Believe me, you son of a bitch, I *will* return the Aqedah to you one day." My smile feels wolfish, like my teeth have thickened into bone crackers and I taste the buttery iron of marrow across my tongue. "I'll return it straight through your cold, black heart."

He chuckles and it is a slithering thing across the skin of my shoulders. "You are going to aim for the black one this time? The others will be so relieved."

"You aren't funny."

"Humor is everywhere."

"It's not."

"You own my knife, but you own no understanding. The universe is one tremendous joke." His hands swirl around as he near dances. "What could be funnier than a starving child? A mother watching her child wasting from hunger, belly swollen with the gasses from the juices within as they eat away the lining for lack of even a bite of food, unable to save them? Ah!" A raw red finger juts to the sky. "The truest joke played in this life! A mother watching her child starve to death while she has more food than she could ever eat."

His words crawl across my brain and I feel the pang of hunger like a knot in my belly that hangs from the back of my throat.

I shake my head and mutter, "*Fucking elder gods.*"

"Excuse me?"

"Nothing." I wave him off. "Just leave her alone and stand there while I try to find this Ship Current."

"Shupnikkurat?"

"Whatever K-I-Y's wifey-bitch is called."

"Ishnigarrab, the Black Goat of the Woods with a Thousand Young, Mother Midnight, Ram with a Thousand Eyes, Crimson Blasphemy, Ten-horn, Lilith, Shub Niggurath . . ." The Man in Black counts off using his red right hand, the fingers gleaming in the moonlight like they are wet, and I realize we are in some kind of pine scrub, the spindly trees spaced far enough apart and stunted enough that weak moonlight falls on us.

Something crawls across my neck, something small with a half-dozen itchy legs.

I swat at it and my fingers come away with a small, hard thing and I realize it's just a ladybug. It crawls up my fingers, struggling with the oily coating of sweat touching my skin has left behind. I shake it off and quit watching it as it falls toward the ground. The air is thick, humidity wrapping my head like a wet towel, making the heat invasive, crawling under the coat, under my clothes until I am damp from head to toe.

Moist.

I hate that fucking word.

It feels dirty in my mouth, dirtier than *fuck* or *shit* or even *cunt*, and I can never say it without feeling like a pervert.

And I hate feeling like a pervert.

The prickly heat makes me feel strange, like things with too many legs are crawling under the coat, and the thought of using my magick again threatens to make my stomach churn.

I take a deep breath.

What must be done, must be done.

Ashtoreth speaks. "I can find her, Charlie."

The Man in Black spits and I swear it sizzles in the carpet of pine needles that covers the ground. "Such a familiar."

His tone makes it sound like an insult.

Ashtoreth ignores him, looking only at me. "With this thing I can help. The Great Mother and I are . . . close. She is near enough that I can lead us to her."

I don't have to use magick? "Okay," I say.

Ashtoreth leans in and her skin glistens with microdots of sweat. I didn't know goddesses could sweat. Her voice is close to a whisper. "You can draw from your fetishes for power."

The word jolts me, shakes me, and my mind rolls it around in growing anger at the intimacy and assumption and I am furious and full of anger at this, this *whore* goddess labeling me.

Who the *hell* does she think she is?

Wait.

Wait.

Fetish. A sexual desire.

Also an object of magickal power.

The coat, the torc, my mark, Oathbreaker, the Aqedah, Cthulhu's gem that remains hidden deep in the folds of the coat.

My *fetishes.*

She moves away before I can apologize for my thoughts.

The Man in Black stares at me.

"What?" I say.

"Our little goddess is very helpful to you."

"That's what friends do."

He smirks.

"What?"

"Nothing, Charlotte Tristan Moore, but perhaps we should follow your oh, so helpful friend before she disappears."

Looking around, I find Ashtoreth has moved far enough away that I have a hard time picking her out of the darkness. She is cresting a small hill about thirty feet away, all softly gleaming skin and darkness melding hair. A trail of clothes lies behind her, skirt crumpled on the ground like a shed skin, blouse swaying on a scrawny pine branch that bounces with its weight. Ashtoreth is naked as she drops down the other side of the short bluff and I can't see her anymore.

As I move after her Nyarlathotep falls in behind me and I wonder if when I catch up to her will she still be naked or will she have manifested some new form with clothes and everything?

"We shall see, Coatbearer," the Man in Black mutters from nearly beside me. "We shall see."

51

THE ANSWER IS clothes.

Mostly.

The bluff is troublesome to climb, the pine needles sliding underfoot on a bed of gritty red clay and threatening to knock you on your skull. The coat helps me stay upright by stretching to lash itself to pine scrub or brace me from tilting too far over my center of gravity; if it didn't then I'd fall and tumble and wind up skull knocked.

The Man in Black walks as if it were a summer afternoon and he had not a care in the world, as if the ground were smooth and paved under his feet, and I hate him for my struggle.

If anyone would be at home in the darkness it'd be him.

The other side of the bluff is a steep ridge that drops away for about fifty feet. The pine needles lie in pockets around rocks like silvery puddles. The exposed dirt is weirdly bright brown, orange tinted in the moonlight.

Ashtoreth is already at the bottom of the ridge, standing on the edge of a gravel lot that holds a large ramshackle building with a sheet metal roof. She has some kind of multi-coloured ribbony thing that lies on her body like streamers at a child's birthday party.

I look past her and study the building in the gravel lot. The wall toward us is dark from the ground to about halfway up in a strange undulating wave pattern. A handful of smaller shacks lean around the back of the building, standing but not straight, all with very similar metal roofs. In the center of the main building is a black pipe spewing a steady stream of gray smoke that swirls through the air and settles around the building like a shroud of spider silk.

The Man in Black is close and leans closer.

"Traitor," he whispers.

The coat screams in my head, and even though I don't understand its language, I know a "fuck you" when I hear it.

The Man in Black mutters something I don't understand and is suddenly gone from beside me in a swirl of darkness. One moment there, the next gone, and I choke on the rotten egg stench of sulfur. He stutters back into existence down the ridge beside Ashtoreth, looming above her. She takes a quick step away and he leans toward her.

If he hurts her . . .

The coat trills across the back of my brain and the noise of it calls out Ashtoreth's words.

You can draw from your fetishes for power.

Okay.

I reach inside the coat and my right hand goes numb and tingly from the cold that envelops it. I think about it and my fingers brush the dry silk of the ribbons around Oathbreaker's handle. I close them, but I don't pull it out. I don't trust it. I don't know how to do this, to do what Ashtoreth said I could do. I roll magick from the center of me down into my Mark and it grows warm.

There is a tug as Oathbreaker responds. It reminds me of fishing with my father as a small girl, when my world was all innocence and summer days, before that night, before the trial, and *way* before the Man in Black and this elder-god-end-of-the-world bullshit. I'd sit next to my dad, glad to be there beside the lake, looking out over the water, holding the fishing pole he had baited for me, watching the end of it for movement. Long hours of him and me and the summer heat and the green smells and the soft jazz playing over the small radio he kept in his tackle box until, suddenly, the pole would bend and the line would jerk, as a fish took the bait and ran.

That hit and tug is how it feels when Oathbreaker goes for my magick but inside my skin and in the middle of my limb like it was a hollow tube of nothing but etheric energy and spacevoid. The skin of my palm itches and they begin drawing my magick into them.

Oh, that's not how this is going to work.

I let the etheric energy spool into Oathbreaker and my neck tickles as their excitement grows.

Just a little more . . .

I grit my teeth against the red lust that wants to subsume me. It builds as pressure in my sinuses and it slithers through the destructive anger that is a part of me, that has been a part of me since that life-shattering night so long ago.

The part of me that could slaughter the entire world.

Oathbreaker vibrates in my hand as they suck in more of my magick, more of my essence.

There.

I clamp down and with a snap of my will turn my magick into a barbed thing.

Spines of etheric energy sink into Oathbreaker's power and it bucks as they realize what I have done. They fight, but I fight harder. I am an autonomous entity. They are an inanimate object. My will is stronger and I reel my magick back into myself, bringing along the essence of Oathbreaker with it. They cry out and it tingles under my skin as their essence enters me like a surge of strength.

Next time give yourself freely to your Mistress and it won't hurt.

Wait. Those words aren't mine. They are, but I wouldn't threaten pain for compliance.

Would I?

The command works and Oathbreaker stops struggling against me. I pull their magick into me until I am full and then cut it off sharply.

I feel strong. I feel good.

I feel absolutely amazing.

The sticky night air doesn't bother me anymore, I can sense everything, even the molecules of oxygen and hydrogen clinging to one another in microscopic dots on my skin, and everything around me has a clarity that almost cuts my vision.

I look down at Ashtoreth and Nyarlathotep and make a small wish.

52

I AM SUDDENLY beside them.

No stinging rain inside my skin, no brick in my stomach. Just one moment there, the next here.

Maybe it's the short distance, but I think it's more the boost I got from Oathbreaker. So much buzzing magick inside me that the small teleportation didn't suck me dry. Didn't even make a dent.

I could get used to this.

Ashtoreth and Nyarlathotep stand to my right, both watching the building.

I'm about to ask, *What are we waiting for?* when I feel the *hum* in the air in front of us.

It buzzes ever so slightly just on the edge of the gravel that lies just a few inches from the tips of my boots.

"What is that?"

Ashtoreth doesn't turn when she replies. "A ward."

"Will it keep us out? Or just tell them we're here?"

The Man in Black says, "Neither."

"What does it do then?"

"To you? Nothing."

"To you?"

"It will keep us."

"It's a trap?"

"It is."

"Strong enough to hold you?" I'm not being sarcastic; I know the Crawling Chaos is powerful, insanely so. He's a primal elder god for Christ's sake. I don't know if I can even truly conceive of all he is and so I don't try. I keep him compartmentalized in my mind so I can deal with the reality of him.

He ignores me.

Ashtoreth answers. "It holds the Great Mother; it can hold almost any of us."

"Can it hold all three of you?" I ask. "That's a lot of elder god to corral."

"I am not an elder god," she replies.

"Still"—I drop my voice into a Firefly/Captain Mal drawl, playing for a little humor toward her—"you ain't nothing and that's sure something."

She doesn't smile. Probably not getting it. "I am not enough to tip the scales in this ward."

"I wasn't trying to make you feel bad."

"Thank you."

I stare at the building with them for a long moment. "Shub Nizzle-nazzle is in there though."

The Man in Black growls at my mispronunciation. "Therein lies our quandary."

I step forward in one long stride. The ward feels about as thick as a piece of paper, just a line of magick that moves through me as I step over, vibrating the bones in my foot, then my shin, my thigh, throughout my torso, and up into my teeth, until I am on the other side of it. The fillings in my molars ache and the gravel crunches underfoot as I turn and face them. "Wait here. I'll go see what's what."

"We cannot do that, Charlotte Tristan Moore." It's almost a snarl coming from his mouth.

"Why not? Let me go try to break this ward."

He lifts his red right hand, the fingers splayed out as it hangs before me, just skimming the edge of the ward, creating a magickal feedback loop that spikes the pain in the back of my mouth. The gold chain dangles off his wrist, swaying as he swings his hand back and forth. "I have been sent. I must go. There is no not-going."

I step back, moving away from the feedback, and the ache lessens, still there but not feeling like my teeth are going to crack into shards.

"Then come on. Ashtoreth can stay here."

She blinks. "Whither thou goest I go."

"It's okay. Stay."

Her energy spikes and she shifts from foot to foot as her hands rub each other like fighting cats. The white ribbons she has for clothes swing around her, opening and closing as she moves faster and faster in an anxious jitter. Tears leak from her dark eyes, sliding along her cheeks.

She's losing her shit.

"Hey, hey," I say softly, "it's okay. It's all right."

"Don't, don't, don't, please . . ." Her voice is small, constricting on itself. "Don't leave me alone out here."

I step over and reach for her. "It's okay."

She falls forward into me and my arms wrap around her. The coat swoops to surround us and I'm holding a fallen love goddess like a child who had a nightmare.

And she's inside the ward.

The Man in Black echoes my thoughts as if he read them. The word is shocking in its profanity as he says, "Fuck."

He steps across the line onto the gravel.

Across the lot behind me a door opens, slamming into a wall with a *bang*!

53

Two MEN AND a woman stand by the door to the building across the lot from us. The one in the center jerks his head in our direction and they all begin walking toward us in a crunch of gravel under boot heels.

They are all carrying guns.

This isn't good.

I push Ashtoreth off and behind me, turning to face the trio head-on.

The coat trills in my head and flutters around me, pressing Oathbreaker's hilt against my ribs so I know where to reach for it. I'm magick with a cursed sword, a living coat made of archangel skin, and two gods as my backup against three people who look like factory-issue humans with guns.

Should be no contest.

But this elder god chase I've been on has taught me that nothing is as it seems, and these three off-the-rack humans are moving with a lot of confidence.

And I know they already have one elder god in captivity.

I shift my stance, widening my feet for stability on the gravel, and shake my arms to loosen them up. The coat pulls its lapel up off my chest just enough that if I go for it I can get Oathbreaker out with as little loss of speed as possible.

The crunching gets louder as they get closer. The men could be related. The one in the front is tall and rangy, with a lumberjack beard that has enough silver that I can see it in the moonlight. His hair loops around bigger ears and curls along his shoulders, not fashionably but in a lack-of-haircut way. The beard and the hair make it to where all I can really see of his face is a nose and brow that both jut forward like the place an iceberg has sheared itself off a glacier, and a pair of eyes so deepset they glow almost white in moonlight like phosphorus in a cave. He stalks rather than walks, using an easy gait that eats distance and still looks casual, almost a swagger. He's dressed in dark clothes, jeans and a T-shirt. The way he holds the shotgun in his hands pulls the short sleeves up over significant biceps and I can see the white skin at their edge gleaming.

Farmer's tan.

The other man is the younger version of him, a little more muscular, beefy where the first man is more gristle and bone, and cooler, his hair pulled into a loose topknot and the one arm holding his pistol tattooed in a design I can't read, but it's big and colourful. He walks with less confidence, leaning forward like he's pushing his way through something instead of having the I-own-this-room assurance of the first man. I'd guess son, but he might be younger brother or even nephew.

He's a sidekick, backup, still dangerous, but the first man is the one to watch.

The girl is a total wild card.

She's short, shorter than me by a good bit, and pretty. Not just average pretty but nearly stunning, with a heart-shaped face and wide almond eyes. Her hair eats the moonlight, blending in with the shirt that binds the curves of her tightly. She's a step or two behind the men because of her shorter stride, not because of any subservience; that is writ plainly across her face and the line of her shoulders as she marches holding some kind of stubby rifle at waist level. I don't know what it is, but it looks like something that can spit a lot of bullets in a short amount of time. The look on her face says she may not wait for the first man to act.

I speak to Nyarlathotep from the side of my mouth. "Be ready for anything."

He chuckles. "I am the Crawling Chaos; anything is the entire realm of my possibility, Charlotte Tristan Moore."

The three of them stop about eight feet away, far enough that their guns are effective but more than a little outside the reach of my sword if I draw it.

The first man raises his chin. "Charlotte? That's your name?"

"Charlie." I tilt my head toward the Man in Black. "Nobody calls me Charlotte but him. Who're you?"

"Ephraim." I can hear a southern drawl lurking behind his pronunciation, saying "Eff-rum" with a roll on the last syllable. "You human?"

"Mostly. Who's with you?"

"Caleb and Malice Wonderland."

"Really?" I can't help but smile at this. I look at the woman. "Middle initial's *N*, I assume."

Malice raises the rifle to her shoulder. "Fuck you, *Charlotte*." She spits my name like it's an insult.

Ephraim smiles. "Thank you for bringing us two new gods to add to our menu."

I feel Ashtoreth's hand on my back through the coat and I know she's touching me to comfort herself, not to reassure me.

"Nope. We're here to take the one you have."

"Oh, that isn't going to happen, girlie."

"Don't call me girlie. We aren't scared of your guns." Not true, but you don't ever admit fear to your opponent.

Ephraim laughs. "Haven't you noticed the Crawling Chaos is weirdly silent?"

I glance over at the Man in Black. He stands, tall and angular, hands tucked into the pockets of his suit, and unnaturally still, like a thing carved of basalt in the moonlight.

The coat rustles around me, its agitation a running murmur in my brain.

"He knows this ain't no ordinary shotgun, darlin'."

I barely have time to turn and try to protect Ashtoreth as he swings the gun up and fires at my head.

54

Ashtoreth grunts as I drive her to the gravel with my body. My ears close from the thunder of the shotgun blast and heat runs across my back. I push off her and roll, coming up with the help of the coat even as it cries out in my brain. I have Oathbreaker in my hand before I'm fully standing. Its hunger surges inside me and I lunge toward the closest enemy.

I'm face-to-face with Ephraim.

I swing Oathbreaker up, aiming to shear through his waist and spill his entrails on the gravel below. Oathbreaker wants to see what his intestines look like dipped and battered in tiny pieces of granite. Ephraim jumps away, swinging the shotgun like a bat, and the edge of the sword *kerrangs* off the steel barrel. Oathbreaker howls and I feel it inside my chest. Ephraim swings the shotgun toward me. I step inside his guard and twist, driving my left arm under his, knocking the gun up as he pulls the trigger.

A gout of blue fire spews into the night air.

What the fuck was that?

Heavy yellow smoke falls like soot and all I can smell is rotten eggs. Sulfur.

Did that shotgun just shoot hellfire and brimstone?

These thoughts roll together as I pivot and swing Oathbreaker, aiming to take his leg off below the knee.

I feel the sledgehammer punch of the bullets hitting the coat before I hear the chatter of Malice's gun.

The hit skews me sideways, spoiling my strike, and I go to one knee. The chatter keeps going and I keep getting punched in the back. The coat screams as it absorbs the bullets, saving my life, but it feels like someone is taking a baseball bat to my spine. All the air drives from my lungs and my diaphragm convulses, hitching my lungs up into my throat.

Oathbreaker falls from my hand and I can't even try to hold on to it.

It only lasts a few seconds, but it is a few seconds that leaves me with no breath and with shards of agony lancing into my whole body.

The coat weeps around me and I suck in air, trying to get enough to get back up, and I wait for the killing blow to fall on me while I am helpless.

I look up and see the Man in Black has become a thing of teeth and tentacles and barbed quills. He's a shapeshifter. I've seen him in a form like this, his true form through my magick, and as an arachnidesque creature. I know he can do it, but the transformation is so horror-movie-special-effects that it still makes everything in me jump. He flows across the gravel and wraps around Caleb, the son/brother/nephew, lifting him off his feet and squeezing him. Caleb's eyes bulge and his face goes dark as he beats at the chaos god who has him like a python has a rabbit.

What once was the Man in Black's face rears back, jaw slewing sideways to reveal many rows of jagged enamel that gleam wetly.

Ephraim steps up and fires a blast of hellfire into that mouth.

The Man in Black rolls backward, carrying Caleb with him.

Ephraim shouts something in a language that sparks turquoise from his mouth, and moves the shotgun in a pattern that feels like some kind of spell.

I push myself up to move toward him, pain pulling tight across my kidneys, when Ashtoreth screams my name.

I turn and find Malice putting another clip into her rifle.

The coat drags around me, hurt. I spin on my heel and move to close the distance to the immediate threat. Malice seats the clip and racks the slide before I can take a second step. Her lovely face is a snarl as she points the rifle at me. The coat tries to wrap around me, pulling across my chest, but it's struggling and I don't think it will be able to save me.

My eyes squeeze tight, waiting for the gut-tearing punch of bullets.

Ashtoreth is there behind Malice, hands slipped around the girl's torso, cupping her breasts as she bites Malice just over her jugular. Malice's eyes roll back and her hands drop, gun falling from loose fingers to clatter on the ground. Ashtoreth pulls back as I step up. Teeth marks stand out on Malice's skin, pulsing with the blood flow beneath them. Her eyes blink rapidly as she comes out of her swoon.

"Wha—" is all she gets out before I clip her hard on her little chin with an uppercut that would make my boxing coach grin from ear to ear.

She drops like someone teleported all the bones out of her body.

The collar tightens around my throat and I push that thought away before my treacherous magick makes it happen.

Ashtoreth's eyes are wide. "That blow was . . . *impressive.*"

The way she says the word makes me feel things deep in my stomach. Things warm and fluttery and uncomfortable in their pleasure.

I turn away to help the Man in Black.

I catch a small glimpse of him, back in his man form and wrapped in black bands of etheric energy on the ground, before the butt of Ephraim's shotgun puts out my lights.

55

JESUS FUCK, MY head is killing me.

Jesus fuck, my back *is killing me.*

I hurt from my waist to the top of my head.

My silent head. There's no background noise and my thoughts ping around in a hollow.

The ache is made worse for how cold I am.

I smell iron.

Not metal iron, but blood iron.

And something else.

Iron and . . . woodsmoke?

I open my eyes and find I am in a large room. The floor I'm lying on is hard and slick and in a pattern of squares that used to be black and white, but the black is scratched to a weird gray and the white has gone off to the colour of cake batter. I know this; it's linoleum. Cheap linoleum that has been kept well past its expiration date.

"You may as well rise, Charlotte Tristan Moore. They are aware that you have woken."

It's the voice of the Man in Black.

I take his cue and sit up. Every bit of that hurts like hell. I feel bruised inside my body, as if the organs of the middle part of me are all swollen and sloshy with fluid. I shiver and it shakes the pain loose, letting it rattle around. In the short distance from the floor I move from chill into warmth.

Ephraim is throwing wood into a pit.

The pit is surrounded by a short brick wall that throws a wide shadow across the floor from the glowing orange light that spills from the center of it. Each time he tosses a gnarled piece of wood in, sparks flit out like gnats that have been lit afire and set free to dash and dance until they are consumed, immolated into nothingness. He looks to be arranging the wood carefully and as he adds each piece the glow intensifies and it bathes his face until he appears to be an abstract painting of himself, all sunset tones surrounded by black silhouettes where his beard and hair frame his craggy features; the light smooths him out, making his features less harsh. With the dim light, all I can see is his face and arms, the middle of him soaking in the darkness, everything else lost in shadows. It doesn't help that the room is cast in smoke from the pit, which gives everything a surreal feeling.

And my fucking head is fucking killing me.

Around me comes a rhythmic thrumming, like the air is moving back and forth slowly.

Where is my coat?

In my head I jerk around to look for it.

My body rebels and I move as if I am suspended in syrup, and even the short motion brings another flash of pain.

I go back to watching Ephraim.

Satisfied with his work, he straightens and steps away, into the darkness. Beyond where he was is something I cannot make out as my eyes haven't adjusted yet. Noises come from the dark. Metal noises. Ephraim returns holding a large metal grate. It's round like the pit, big enough that I could lie on it like a bed and my feet would not hang off. Three pipes about as long as my forearm jut from the underside of it. At that size the thing must weigh well over a hundred pounds, but Ephraim carries it as if it weighs nothing. He drops it into the pit legs first, raising a storm of sparks and smoke.

Dusting off his hands, he moves around the pit toward me. "Glad you're awake. *Charlie,* wasn't it?"

I don't answer.

The Man in Black does. "That is what her friends call her."

"Well, I may not be a friend, but *Charlie* it is."

I swallow to speak. "Where's my coat?"

"Thought you might miss that old rag." He moves away, growing dim in the shadows. After a moment I hear a click and a buzz and fluorescent lights flicker on overhead.

Oh hell.

What the actual fuck?

The room is a nightmare full of nightmares and my brain cannot keep up with it all, can't process it, just stutters around it like a man with his foot cut off trying to cross the street.

Around me are stainless-steel appliances so common they immediately slide into my head in easily categorized slots.

Refrigerator, stove, deep fryer, prep table, oven.

I'm in a kitchen. An industrial kitchen. Like in a restaurant. Like the one at Mama Mia's Pizzeria where I worked through college, not the same but close enough that I know it without much need to process it.

The Man in Black stands upright to my left, hands chained above his head to a shackle-bolt embedded in the wooden rafters that hold up the roof.

Ashtoreth sits in a chair of some kind, wrapped in something that looks very much like blue plastic wrap. She's slumped forward, out cold.

These things all scramble around in my brain, finding their spots because I can recognize them without thought, which is good because the rest of my mind boggles like a squeeze toy in the hand of a drunk child at the thing across the pit from me.

I cannot close my eyes, can't force the lids shut; I can only stare, trying to make sense of the thing chained to a steel rack that looks like a cross between a medieval torture rack and a gynecological exam table built in the depths of hell itself by some nightmare demon version of the Marquis de Sade. Blades and bars jut from it haphazardly and chains with hooks dangle from the edges where they have pulled free from the thing bound on its surface, their tips glistening black and red in the flickering hum of the overhead fluorescent.

On the table is a massive creature made of horns and fur and breasts and hooves and eyes. She has a head that vaguely looks like a goat with a snout and muzzle and beard, topped by long spirals of chitin that form a crown of horn, the wicked points gleaming as high above her brow as a small child could stand. Her eyes, the ones on her face, not the ones that dot her black-furred body—those have no lids and lie bare and pale and iris-less in clusters like spider eggs—are squeezed shut into wrinkled pockets the size of my face and her lips pull back to reveal hard rows of yellow teeth that interlock together like the splintered ends of a tree struck by lightning. Her arms are pulled back, shackled to the rack, exposing a chest and torso double lined with swollen breasts that thrust out of the coarse fur that covers the rest of her body; their skin is thin, laced with throbbing varicose tubes of blood that make a lattice around each one and trace their way up to the peaks of chapped nipples, the skin there cracked and flaking with each breath she draws and releases. Viscous fluid runs from them in rivulets, pulsing out and trailing down the sloped sides to soak into the fur around her belly in widening glossy patches. It drips under her into a row of glass jars and is the not-quite-bone off-white colour of condensed milk. Multiple legs, triple jointed and capped with heavy hooves, run the side of her torso and each of them is also shackled and pulled back with chains to expose a vulva as long as my leg and pulsing as if being pumped full of air.

My brain clicks, flipping switches into logic so I can function again.

Shupnikkurat.

Shub Niggurath.

Great Mother.

Black Goat of the Woods with a Thousand Young.

As I stare, her stomach convulses and a shape rolls from one side of it to another under the stretched-too-thin skin and the impression from underneath is of horn and teeth and hooves. The movement draws out a cry from her that stabs into the meat of me, driving through my sternum to puncture my chest, and the hollow, mournful nature of that sound bangs against the inside of my ribs like the fists of something I don't recognize trapped there and trying to pummel and thrash their way out of the cage that is my chest. She shudders and the cry drains away, falling down my body to the floor, and as it washes over me I begin to weep for the unborn children I never wanted.

56

"WHY ARE YOU crying, little girl?"

The voice makes me turn toward Ephraim and the sight of him in the light fills me with a hot rage and it makes me stand to my feet. There is a chain wrapped around my ankle and locked in place. It trails from me to one of the steel tables where it is locked around the leg of it as well. *Two legs chained to each other.* "I'm not your goddamn 'little girl.'"

He's covered by a wide apron that hangs from his neck, the dark cloth of it stitched or painted with symbols and sigils that make my eyes hurt more than the overhead lights. I've seen markings like them before tracing the hem of a robe worn by an evil high priest of some cult that had Cthulhu in a fish tank and cut pieces of him off to serve to customers in the sushi restaurant that sat above.

Wait.

Kitchen.

Fire pit.

Elder goddess in chains.

Oh hell.

"What is this place?"

The Man in Black answers, "It is what you fear it is."

Ephraim laughs, a big belly laugh, making the apron shift, and I see that he has the shotgun that throws hellfire slung around his shoulders and chest.

And he has Oathbreaker slid through the belt around his waist.

"Black Oak Barbeque," he says, "home of absolutely *otherworldly* brisket."

His teeth shine through his beard.

I don't take my eyes off Ephraim, not with him having two weapons, as I address the Man in Black. "What is it with people eating your kind?"

He shrugs and it makes the shackles on his wrists clink. "Humanity has always sought to devour deity."

"He's right," Ephraim says. "Hell, the Catholics have been munching down on Jesus for two thousand years." He spits into the pit in a long stream and it sizzles as it hits the coals. "Fuckin' blasphemers."

"You do know you have a fertility goddess, a chaos god, and a love goddess right here, don't you?"

"So?"

I shake my head. "Seems like you would be the blasphemer."

His bright eyes narrow. "You some kind of Bible-thumper?"

"Yes, I thump the Bible every night and pray to sweet baby Jesus for the souls of my enemies." The sarcasm drips from my mouth like poisoned honey.

His face pinches closed and his voice is a snarl. "Mouthy little bitch."

I ignore the insult and answer him straight. "I know someone who is a believer."

"Her lover," the Man in Black offers.

"Thought that was you."

We both laugh and it feels taffy-stretch strange to be in sync with Nyarlathotep.

Ephraim looks at us sideways. "Where's he at? He some kind of pussy to leave you to do the fighting?"

"Don't worry about him."

"I'm not. If he comes here after you I'll just add him to the menu."

Does he mean that literally?

Looking in his eyes, I am sure he does. "That's cannibalism."

"And?" he asks. "What do you think your fate is?"

I hadn't thought about it, not like that.

He smiles. "Yeah, darlin', tomorrow when this place has a line of followers a half mile long you will be the appetizer for their main course. I think you'll make a fine Brunswick stew."

The fact that he calls me darlin' makes me flinch inside and echoes of words said long ago ricochet in my skull: *It's okay, darlin'; just stop struggling, darlin'; you're going to hurt yourself;* and finally, after he hit me so hard my jaw dislocated, *This is happening, darlin', so lay the fuck still and take it.* I fight to keep it off my face as I clamp down on the fear goblin that word sets loose inside me, shunting it aside and focusing on the part I need here and now. My voice is strained in my ears, but the sentence I spit out is complete. "There'll be that many people here tomorrow?"

"Every day that ends in a *y*."

"You make a lot of money selling godflesh?"

Ephraim laughs. "What good is it for a man to gain his soul and lose all the profit in the world?"

"You run this by yourself?"

"You sure are a curious kitten." He scratches under the edge of his beard.

"When's the next time you'll get to brag?"

"Why would I do that?"

I play the card. "You have enough ego to capture a fertility goddess. I figure you have enough ego to want to tell people about it."

He looks down at me and I see him contemplating.

"I would listen to the tale," the Man in Black says.

Ephraim turns to him. "You don't already know?"

The Man in Black shrugs, making his chains sound against each other. "Obviously I am not omniscient."

Ephraim nods. "Point taken."

He shifts his position, settling in on himself, and I know we're about to hear a story.

57

"THERE HAVE BEEN Montreaux in this holler since the Pilgrims."

Ephraim has reached under his apron and pulled out a pouch of some sort. He unzips it and a gnarled thing falls out into his hand. It takes a moment for me to recognize it as a pipe. I watch as he taps it against the inside of the pit and then blows on it. It's made from some dark twisty chunk of wood and has a long stem. He pulls something from the pouch in four pinches, taking each bit from his fingertips and shoving it into the pipe, using the pad of his thumb to press it into place.

Finally satisfied, he reaches into the pit again and comes out with a red-hot coal held between his fingers. He sticks the pipe in his mouth and the coal in the bowl of the pipe. His cheeks bellow in and out as he draws a deep lungful and holds it.

He exhales a long stream of white smoke that stays low, separate from the light gray smoke rising from the pit. It sweeps over my face and immediately drops to the very bottom of my lungs. My mouth is full of a dank, sticky-sweet flavor.

Cannabis.

Weed.

Mary, ju wanna?

I recognize it from the period in my younger days, not long after that night, when I ran to the oblivion drugs had for me. Weed wasn't strong enough to make me forget, but it was always at Thom's house, being his chief source of income.

He'd stay baked all day and sell weed to most of the folks who came to him and toss in a couple of joints if they were picking up something harder or pricier, telling them it was "for later, man, so you can mellow after you jolt." Like he was the Hippie-Jesus-of-the-Blessed-Herb spreading the word of the THC god.

Sweet Thom, so stoned he never realized I was only there for the drugs and was never going to put out. He never pressed the issue, never tried or even pushed me on it. Maybe I was so stoned I didn't realize he knew that even that would have broken me.

Huh.

It all seems a little clearer to me now.

I wonder—

STOP!

I crash that thought, short-circuiting it before the connection completes and my magick and the treacherous torc around my throat can kick and wish Thom to this place.

Point is, I never did find a way to like the smell of it.

Ephraim holds the pipe out toward me and grunts around a lungful of smoke. "Wanna hit it?"

I shake my head.

"More for me."

"You did not ask the rest of us," the Man in Black says.

"Humans only." He takes a long pull off the pipe.

And sits there, holding in the smoke.

"Please tell me you don't tell stories like a pothead," I say.

"You're not going to talk in tiny, broken sentences between hits and ramble from some 'time of the Pilgrims' we don't give a shit about and probably never get to the point."

He blows smoke between his teeth. "Heard a high story or two, have you?"

"Never one that I gave a shit about."

Another hit. "You don't want to know how we came to be?"

"Not particularly."

Ephraim turns, shifting to face the Man in Black. "She's ornery, ain't she?"

"You have no idea, human."

"That why she ain't yours anymore?"

"It is a long story."

"Speaking of . . ." He shifts back to me and hits the pipe again. He speaks and his voice is strained, pulled tight to talk and hold the smoke in his lungs. "The Montreaux family has a long history in the Old Country of seeking out his"—he tilts his head toward the Man in Black—"kind and securing power from them. When we came to the New World we found more of his kind that had been here already. Ancient gods who stalked this raw, primitive land, mostly the ones with an affinity for it. We took a few small ones, but once I found the spoor of that one." He tilts his head toward the fertility goddess chained on the other side of the pit. Through the smoke she appears to be a mass of darkness decorated with spots of colour where the firelight gleams off wet eyes and hard horn. "I gathered the family and we hunted her down."

"How did you take such a prey?" the Man in Black asks.

"We waited until her time was upon her and took her in the midst of birth, when she is her most vulnerable."

"Still a pack of rats trying to take a tiger."

"A pack of rats with both *Le Grimoire d'Heliographe* and *Járngreipr.*"

The Man in Black grunts.

"Those are bad, right?" I ask. If it makes the elder god of chaos grunt in surprise they must be.

Ephraim chuckles. "*Járngreipr*, or 'Iron Grippers' if you translate, are the gloves that allowed Thor to wield Mjolnir."

"Wait." I shake my head. "Thor, the god of thunder, is real?"

"Was."

"Was?"

"You think he hit some hard times, maybe divorced Sif, got behind on alimony, and started gambling and pawned off his magickal gloves that let him hold on to anything for a couple ounces of gold and a pint of cheap whiskey?" Ephraim's eyes glitter with mockery. "He was killed and his gloves taken off his corpse before it cooled."

It pisses me off. "So that's your smartass way of saying you killed a storm god?"

He chuckles. "Not me personally."

"Okay, what's the other thing you said?"

"The Helhammer Grimoire is the forbidden text that taught us how to hold gods against their will."

"Did you pick that up at a flea market in Katmandu for a nickel?" I can be a smartass too.

"My great-aunt Clarice strangled two popes to secure it for the family."

The Man in Black pipes up. "Stephen the Sixth and Leo the Fifth were at your hand?"

Ephraim nods and pulls on his pipe. Nothing happens. He leans back and scoops up another coal and relights it.

I have to ask. "Who are they?"

"Two popes in succession; both died of strangulation. Stephen is best known for the Cadaver Synod," Ephraim answers around his mouthful of smoke.

"Sounds ominous."

"He exhumed the rotting corpse of his predecessor, Formosus, and put it on trial, forcing a new-minted deacon to channel the dead bishop for cross-examination." He chuckles. "Nobody does necromancy like the Holy See."

"Popes doing death magick?"

"All the time. If you think about it, the ceremony of Catholicism is a form of it. Revering a dead man, praying to him, seeking power and hope from him, looking for resurrection or security after death."

"Man, you got a real thing with Catholics, don't you?"

"They killed a lot of my family since the Inquisition."

"What does this have to do with necromancy?"

"The point of necromancy is to beat death, own it, and make it your bitch."

I can see that. He makes a point. "When was this?"

He hits the pipe and his eyes drift up as he tries to remember.

"Leo died in the year 904," the Man in Black supplies.

"What was Leo known for?"

"Mostly for being strangled to death."

"I think that would do it for a pope."

The Man in Black chuckles. "The early church fathers killed each other with frequency. Many of them died violently."

"Huh," I grunt. "Who knew?"

"Historians."

Ephraim brays at this, his laughs turning into choking coughs.

"Nobody likes a smartass," I say.

"That was some funny shit," Ephraim says. "Especially coming from such a dour god like him."

The Man in Black tilts his head. "She and I were discussing my humor just outside of your ward earlier."

"She doesn't think you're funny at all, I take it?"

"She fails to appreciate the joke her existence is." The Man in Black shrugs. "It is one of her shortcomings."

I move, making the chain attached to me rattle loudly. "Enough talking like I'm not right here."

They both look at me.

Time to get back on track and figure out a way to get free.

"So, you have a book, some gloves, and a shitty barbeque joint in the middle of nowhere. What's the point?"

Ephraim drops his pipe into a pocket on his apron. "I also have my Baphomatic 12-gauge pump shotgun—"

"That's the gun that spits fire?"

He nods. "You'll allow the clever title as it is mine." His fingers drop and brush the handle of my sword at his waist. "And now I have Oathbreaker." He points at me. "And once we start the butchering of you I'll have that fancy bit of jewelry around your throat. I don't know what it is, but I bet it ain't a fashion accessory."

I swallow and feel the metal torc against my throat.

If he finds a way to use the magick of the torc he will be able to find more gods, wish them here to his wards, and keep building his power.

I don't know what his game is and I don't care; we've talked enough for me to know that Ephraim having more power is not a good thing. He's a collector of magick objects.

Oh shit.

"Where's my coat?"

Inside my coat are the Aqedah and the soul gem of Cthulhu and who knows what else. I don't know what Ephraim could do with any of it, but again, nothing good.

He points to one of the tables and there sits a box made of some form of clear glass and held shut by a flip clasp with a pin in it. Darkness roils around inside it, slamming against the walls of it and folding back into itself to try again. Each time it throws itself against the lid the clasp of it jiggles, but the pin stays firmly in place.

He steps to it, places his hand on the lid, and touches the pin.

The darkness goes crazy.

It thrashes and flails and from the box comes a high-pitched whine that makes the teeth in the back of my mouth ache because I feel it more than hear it and it makes me acutely aware that I don't have the voice of the coat in my mind and the loss of it cuts like a glass shard.

He pulls the pin with blunt fingers, keeping his other palm flat on the top of the box. Once the pin is removed, the clasp falls and the lid rises just a crack, but it is enough for the whine to blossom in my brain as a wild alien scream of longing and fear and anger and it all wraps my head like a wet towel and I recognize the voice, the one I have lived with for weeks now, lived with it babbling at me anytime I am awake.

The coat surges out of the paper-thin opening in a long ribbon, spooling out in an eyeblink toward me. I lunge toward it, wanting the comfort of it back around me, the protection.

Ephraim slams the lid shut with a grunt.

The ribbon of coat falls from the air, cut off from the host body. It flutters to the floor as Ephraim pushes the pin back in place.

I shout in rage before I realize it.

Box secured, Ephraim picks up the scrap of coat, fingers working to roll it into a tube of blackness. He winks at me and tosses it into his mouth.

He chews and swallows.

"That was just divine, even raw," he says. "I can imagine the crowd will go wild tomorrow if we offer fried Seraphim skin."

The tears are in my eyes. "How could you do that?"

"Cut it into strips, batter it in a buttermilk and egg wash, roll it in flour and salt and pepper, dip it in the wash again, roll it one more time and then into the deep fryer for, oh"—he looks up at the ceiling, calculating—"probably eight minutes."

"I'm going to kill you."

"Not likely, little girl, not unless I choke on my Brunswick stew tomorrow, but I don't anticipate that happening."

Pain sears my ears as the room fills with a spike of howling, undulating sound.

Shupnikkurat screams out and as it fades I turn to look. She jerks in her chains, scooting lower on the rack.

Her stomach rolls.

Her labia convulses, parting like a gigantic flower, and from inside her comes one dripping hoof attached to a long leg as spindly and multi-jointed as a spider's.

Ephraim grins.

"Showtime!"

58

Ephraim is in front of the Black Goat Goddess, one hand clasping the hoof of the leg flailing from her birth canal, the other waving in the air and throwing yellow sparks of etheric energy as he howls out an incantation that turns the air thick like a soup of humidity. It smells electric, the burnt-ozone scent of coitus rising up through the air and rolling out even to where I stand.

"What's happening?" I ask the Man in Black.

He stares eagerly at the scene as it plays out, wicked sharp teeth biting into his lower lip as he watches. "You call it the miracle of birth."

Is he . . . breathy?

Another leg and a weird thing that flails like a tentacle squelch their way out of Shupnikkurat.

Ephraim grunts and leans back, pulling, muttering the incantation through clenched teeth.

"Why are you excited?" I ask.

"There is nothing more chaotic than the birth of a

godchild. Sliding into existence on this realm where it will kick and scream and bite and thrash its will out on the reality around it. It will do everything in its power to form its life into what it wants it to be despite the fact that this reality will be resistant, will oppose the very existence of it from the get." He pulls his eyes away from the spectacle. His face has drawn narrow, almost skullish; the dusky skin goes shiny over the ridges of cheek, chin, and brow. His eyes glitter in their caves, tiny firelights of reflection in a mosaic as if they were segmented like that of a fly. "And it is the culmination of lust we watch, the crescendo of coitus. It . . . *arouses* me."

Ew.

I did not need that information.

His face jerks back toward Ephraim and Shub Niggurath.

A bouquet of spindly legs flail around Ephraim's arms and shoulders, and the sleek haunches they are attached to hang out. Some of the hooves clatter on the floor, beating out an abstract tattoo of sound that is anything but music. The tentacle is a tail, or where a tail should be, and whips around, suckered mouths gaping and closing, slinging amniotic ichor in long, flimsy strings.

I look away, my eyes finding Ashtoreth.

She's awake and weeping, tears the size of my thumbnails rolling down her cheeks and splashing off her jawline, and she makes some low moaning sound that combines with the bang and clatter of the hooves on the floor and the grunting squeal from the fertility goddess giving birth and all of it climbs into me and makes me clench deep inside, not in a sex way, but similar, a hollow ache that settles behind my pelvis in the drum of my empty, never-used uterus.

Jesus *fuck.*

I close my eyes and breathe through it, shutting everything down to get control of my own body, following all the training I did for so many years after that horrible night long ago.

When I open them Ephraim is hauling the offspring free.

It falls to the floor with a squelch and a gush of amniotic fluid that fills the air with the sickly-sweet odor of spoiled honey. It's not much smaller than Ephraim, who looms over it, still holding it up by one leg. It kicks with the others, jerking in his grip and slipping free.

"You're a wriggly little bastard, ain'tcha?!" Ephraim chuckles.

The offspring lurches away, driven by flailing limbs and sliding on the linoleum lubricated by its own afterbirth. It has too many legs to stand, like someone has taken a half-dozen newborn fawns and bound them together as a sick joke. Its face is long and divided above its snout with a ridge of bone. Curling horns form a crown above a pronounced brow line, swooping over and around a scattering of wide almond-shaped eyes that roll about in their sockets full of too much intelligence to not know fear. One side of its face smears across the floor; the other blinks in the fresh light.

It mewls a thin, choking mewl and it almost bends me in half with the raw terror it encapsulates.

Ephraim's hand closes on one of the horns and he hauls the offspring up to his chest as if it weighs nothing.

Oathbreaker glitters in his other hand.

I scream, "No!" and lunge forward, legs driving me toward them.

The shackle on my ankle jerks me short, yanking me to the floor as he slits the offspring's throat in one swift stroke.

He laughs at me as black blood spurts into an arc, leaping from the offspring to strike him across the chest, glistening like black ribbons as it runs down his apron.

Behind him the Black Goat weeps.

As I rise off the floor I am hit with the realization that she isn't screaming or thrashing or reacting anything like a mother should who just watched her child be slaughtered in front of her.

She is defeated. She's seen it too many times and she's given up hope.

This is her existence now, reduced from a goddess of birth and life to a mere meat factory. Giving birth each night to watch that child be killed and cooked and offered up to humans who should worship her, should fear her, should tremble in their own piss and shit if she were to even glance in their direction.

Ephraim tosses the carcass of her offspring into the pit.

She turns her face away as the sparks rise and the heat begins to crackle against the wet fur of her dead child.

Ephraim moves toward Ashtoreth holding the dripping Oathbreaker.

"Time to get started on the other entrees," he says. "So much prepwork."

My eyes lock on his back and I let all the hate for him that is in my heart bring my magick to a boil.

The torc cuts deep into my throat as I let it go and wish like hell.

The magick leaves me in a rush and a blink later the shotgun appears in my hands.

It's heavier than I would have thought. I've never held a shotgun, but I didn't think they would weigh so much.

The wood of the stock is smooth under my palm. It's dark, some kind of black walnut or black oak, and there is a crook to it that fits the web of my thumb and right hand like it was carved there just for me. My fingers wrap securely and comfortably around it and it feels like I have held this gun before. It even feels as if my Mark fits somehow into the form of the stock. The barrel stretches out from there in a dull iron gray and this close to it I can see that it is inlaid with a pattern of symbols and sigils that have been etched as if by minuscule fey hands. The power of them radiates up at me as heat. The slide rests in my left hand and the fingers lie in grooves that feel completely natural for them although mine and Ephraim's hands are nowhere close to the same size.

He turns in my direction as my finger slips over the trigger.

I snarl. "Leave my goddamn friends alone."

My finger pulls.

The shotgun tries to buck out of my hands as it spits a fist-sized blast of fire and brimstone.

Ephraim twists as if he doesn't have a spine, throwing up his hand and screaming some word that isn't English, isn't any language spoken in the last two millennia, and the hellfire from the shotgun, *my shotgun now*, deflects off an invisible shield and pinwheels, whirling away. It smashes against the deep fryer and the oil inside it explodes in a gout that ignites into a dull orange spread of flame along the steel appliances beside it.

Ephraim straightens. "You think you'll be able to use my weapon against me? You think I'd allow that from some cheap little piece of trim who doesn't even know how to use her own magick?"

I rack the slide on the shotgun, like I've seen in movies all my life. Immediately I feel the hellfire inside the gun building, as if I am holding a living thing that just wants to spew combustion.

"You don't even know how to hold that thing, you silly little git." Ephraim sneers. He rolls Oathbreaker in a lazy spin, the black blade gleaming at the edge. "I'm going to come over there and take that thing and when I do—"

Darkness explodes behind him and the Man in Black is just there, looming chest to Ephraim's back. The Man in Black's red right hand clamps on Oathbreaker, plucking it from Ephraim's grip as his left arm comes over Ephraim's shoulder and wraps the man's throat in a choke hold.

Ephraim barely has time to sputter, "Wh, wh, what?" before the cursed black blade slides through his back and out his chest in one long spit of blood that splatters hot and bright crimson across the linoleum at my feet.

59

I DON'T KNOW how the Man in Black freed himself.

How long he had the ability to do it.

If he waited till his moment or if he just finally was able to.

It doesn't matter.

Because he is standing there, spattered in blood, with Oathbreaker in his red right hand.

Fuck.

His eyes slide sideways.

Toward the box that holds the coat.

The coat he used to wear, the skin of an archangel he took and made his slave.

My coat.

I take a step and am jerked short by the chain still on my ankle.

I put the shotgun to my shoulder; the barrel is warm on my cheek and magick crackles like static electricity as my skin touches the tiny swirling glyphs. "*Don't,* motherfucker."

He smiles. "Charlotte Tristan Moore." He doesn't take a step, but he is closer to the coat.

"I said, *don't.*"

"It seems fitting that I would have my mantle again since I have my weapon back."

"Take the sword and fuck off. The coat is off-limits."

"It is not your slave."

"Yours either."

He *tsks* at me. "If poor dead Ephraim could deflect that do you not think I can as well?"

"Move toward me, the coat, or Ashtoreth and we will find out."

"You do not even know what you hold in your hands, Twice-Marked. You have no idea, the potential of that weapon."

"Been there before. I'll figure it out."

"Its former owner"—he points at Ephraim's corpse with the sword—"not this one, the true previous owner, never learned all it was before it drove him insane, and he was the host of a vengeance demon for decades before it found him."

Curiosity rises inside me. I want to ask.

Stay on point. Work, Charlie.

He moves without moving again.

I pull the trigger.

60

THE SHOTGUN KICKS me hard enough to slew me sideways, my feet slipping across the blood-spattered linoleum. I rack the slide as I right myself, my body intuitively working with the new weapon.

The blast of hellfire worked; I didn't hit the Man in Black, but he turns away from the coat.

And turns toward Shub Niggurath in her chains.

Horror dawns on me and I know what he's doing.

I pull the trigger again, racking and pulling and riding the kick, chasing him around the fire pit in the center of the room with blast after blast of hellfire.

His left hand waves at me, the fingers twisting as if they were snakes having sex instead of bones and joints.

The bloody corpse of Ephraim rises in the air and absorbs every fireball.

It jerks as it is struck, doing a horrible shimmy and shake that makes its loose limbs flail, and I hear the blood that sheets the apron dangling from its neck sizzling. It swings as if on strings, some kind of broken fucked-up dead-man puppet/pinata. The hellfire sticks where it strikes and burns, blue balefire licking its way up the body, consuming it like paper in fire. As the flesh burns it blackens and curls.

Behind it the Man in Black is beside the Black Goat Goddess. Still holding the sword, he brushes her cheek with the back of his hand, the left one still outstretched and magickally controlling his corpse shield. The tears of the fertility goddess glisten in the flickering light from Ephraim's burning corpse.

I yank on the chain around my ankle.

Nyarlathotep raises the sword.

Ashtoreth screams.

As I turn the shotgun down to the floor and pull the trigger to destroy the chain that holds me hostage, the Man in Black lets the sword fall like swift and terrible lightning.

The cursed sword cleaves deep into the chest of the captured fertility goddess.

The shotgun blast disintegrates the chain and the concussion of it striking the floor so close stumbles me sideways and the world slews as I struggle to keep my eyes pinned on the Man in Black.

He's elbow deep in the gaping wound he has made, fishing around inside Shub Niggurath as she screams in her chains.

The sucking sound of him pulling his arm free is loud enough to hear over the screams of the goddesses and the burning of Ephraim and the offspring. He holds up something that looks very much like a piece of coral except it is translucent and glows with an indigo light that lays harsh highlights across his saturnine face.

The soul gem of the Black Goat of the Woods with a Thousand Young.

When we worked together he harvested one from Yar Shogura, the cancer god, and one from Cthulhu. He kept the cancer god's, but I wound up with Cthulhu's in our last fight.

If he gets three he can free his father, the Mad God Azathoth, who will eat this world.

He purses his lips and blows across its surface and the dripping ichor from the Black Goat Goddess's body cavity dries to a powder and softly flakes away.

He looks at me and winks.

And disappears with a stuttering out of existence.

61

HE'S GOING AFTER Daniel.

His wink tells me that.

I throw my magick into my scream and wish myself after him as violently as I can.

And nothing happens.

My magick simply surges inside my chest and roils there, unable to connect with the torc that's . . .

My fingers touch my throat.

The torc is gone.

A sound makes me turn.

Ashtoreth stands there, free and crying, oily tears slickening her cheeks. "I'm sorry, Charlie . . ."

In her hand is my torc.

What the hell?

"How are you free?"

"Charlie . . ."

The Man in Black freed himself. Now here is Ashtoreth, free and holding the thing I need to go after him.

"Answer my fucking question, Ashtoreth."

Her head drops to her chest. "Nyarlathotep freed me once he broke the spell that shackled him. It took time, even for him. They know what they are doing here . . ."

My next words spit so hard they make my mouth hurt.

"What did you do?"

"He made me . . ."

Her betrayal hits me like a hammer. Every inch of my skin goes cold with it and my magick turns to ashes in my mouth. There is a circle around my vision, a haze on the edges, and the whole world is on the other side of it. I realize I am holding the shotgun still and it is so heavy I let it fall to only one hand, the barrel clattering against the ground. It drags against my arm as I walk slowly around the guttering fire pit. Ashtoreth reaches toward me as I draw near, but I turn my shoulder to her, my face away, and move past, dragging the gun as I go.

When I reach the glass box on the table, my fingers move on their own and fumble the pin from the latch.

The coat surges out, flinging the lid back, and slithers over me, wrapping itself around me.

My head fills with its song as it flutters and rustles over me, covering me in warmth.

It's okay. It's all right. We're back.

I lift the lapel and push the gun under it. The coat takes it eagerly, storing it away inside itself like it used to do with Oathbreaker.

"Charlie . . ."

I ignore her and turn away. I can't with her, not yet. I have something I have to do. I would have run after the Man in Black, but now that I've been stopped I realize I have to clean this up.

Shub Niggurath blinks up at me from under her horned brow. Her eyes are shaped like the goat she is named after, but the iris and the pupil are strangely human. I don't focus on anything but her eye, ignoring the black fur, the leaking teats, the gaping wound, the gore and ichor and sickly-sweet stench of her, just the eye, peering into her and seeing who and what she is.

Mother.

Like that we are connected, not deeply, but still sharing . . . something.

Warmth leaks from the gash that yawns in her chest, the wound open and empty. She is dying. She won't bear another off-spring in this form on this plane, but she is still an engine of creation, a goddess, and even a wound as great as the one she suffers will take her a long time to die from. And she is suffering from it; I can feel the pain of it through our connection, pulsing between the meat and the skin of me. She *hurts*. She has been hurting, trapped here for a long, long time, at the hands of Ephraim. Knowledge passes between us and I know that before Ephraim it was his father and before that it was his grandfather who held her captive and took her young and made them so much meat for lowly humans to consume.

She wants nothing more than to be free from this bondage.

My hand slides into the pocket of the coat and my Mark crackles as it finds the handle of the Aqedah.

Gently, I lift the chin of the Black Goat of the Woods with a Thousand Young, raising it until I can no longer look her in the eye.

With one swift, sure motion I slit her throat.

I turn away as the life of the form she has now bubbles out onto her chest.

Ashtoreth.

I turn and study her as I walk toward her. Her shoulders droop and she is weeping.

The coat babbles in my mind and a vision of some version of Ashtoreth slides into place.

Her, draped in crimson and purple cloth that forms to her, hugging every lush curve of that form, hair like a raven's wing, face cruelly beautiful, lips swollen from biting and stained with the blood of saints and martyrs. A word blazes out from her forehead as if tattooed there, but I cannot read it. She sits astride a beast, bareback, her thighs pressed to its spine, and it is a magnificent beast, sleek with power and covered in slick fur that blends with her scarlet robes. Its massive shoulders sprout with more than a half-dozen heads that look like a nightmare mix of lion and wolf with mouths full of shark teeth and serpent fangs. Each head has at least one horn, curled and wicked sharp. Blood runs down them to disappear into the fur of the Beast. Ashtoreth sways on its back, lifting a cup and drinking, and laughing as she rides.

Ashtoreth. Shub Niggurath.

The Whore of Babylon and the Beast of the Apocalypse.

I shiver, dissipating the vision.

Her mouth opens as I stop in front of her and I shake my head before she can speak. I reach out and take back the torc, the metal cold to the touch. She doesn't even try to stop me. It hums as I lift it to my head; stretching itself large enough to slip over my face. It is heavy on my collarbones. I let it go and it shrinks itself back to my throat, tightening just slightly for a moment, then settling back to the place I have become so used to it being.

I look at her. "I was your friend."

"I know, I know, I know." Her hair swings around her face as she babbles.

"Why?"

"I didn't want to, Charlie; you have to believe me."

Something inside me breaks.

The edge of the Aqedah is pressed against her throat. The coat follows my mental command and wraps around her, drawing us tight. "Why. Did. You. Do. It?"

"I had no choice; the Son of Azathoth threatened me with—"

I shove her away from me and scream.

The coat unfurls and she stumbles back and falls on her ass. She looks up at me in shock.

I want to gut her, to use the Aqedah and cut her lying face off. I scream again.

Ashtoreth sits and weeps. Her face drops to her hands.

"No!"

She looks up at me sharply.

"Don't you dare look away from me!"

"Charlie . . . I . . ."

"Shut up. Shut the *fuck* up."

She does.

"I never betrayed you. I never left you. I stood up to Hastur and Mylendor and Nyarlathotep for you. I *defended* you from them."

"You would give me over to them for your Daniel." The accusation comes out with an attitude.

"I *didn't*."

"You would have."

"I'd have given them *myself* for Daniel. Not you. Never you."

"You say that, but I know—"

I'm on her, in her face. "You don't know *shit*, not a goddamned thing." Some of my spit hits her in the eye, making her blink rapidly. "I've been at the hands of people who want to use me, to do me harm, to destroy me like I'm some *fucking* toy they can break for their fun. I would *never* leave you at the hands of people like them. *NEVER*." She reels back at the fury I am not even trying to curb, but I press in and keep us close and sink every ounce of menace and threat I can into my next words. "Fix the collar."

Her face turns away from my wrath and I see the pulse of her fear fluttering in her throat and I want to sink my teeth in it and pull it free. Let her bleed out at my feet. Her hand slowly rises, indigo magick crackling off her fingertips, and this close I smell the blackberry and sex scent of it wafting from her goddessflesh.

I want to bite those fingers off.

Teeth crunching through cartilage, wet pop of the joint as it separates, and the gush of salty lymphatic fluid and blood into that hollow under my tongue.

Off.

The fingers dart in, under my chin, and brush the metal ring around my neck. I feel the magick spark and the metal goes hot, buzzing against my skin, and my head swims with everywhere; all the potential for every place I could wish myself to expands my mind and rocks me back on my heels.

Her words filter through the spin of myriadism.

"Charlie, I'm sorry. I want to—"

I hold my hand up, cutting her off. I force my mind back in order, pulling the edges to make them straight, as straight as they can be. I breathe, in through my nose, out through my mouth, and center myself. I search, the collar growing heavy as I do, pushing my magick out, looking, seeking, searching.

I find it.

I draw a breath to make a wish and the coat slaps my face with its collar as it trills in my head.

And I know what it wants me to know.

It's still making gibberish and I don't have an English translation, but I understand. It's saying we need some fuel.

I hold on to the location of the Man in Black and turn to the goddess of betrayal.

She reaches up as I move to her, hands lifted in supplication. "I'll make it up to you, Charlie. Anything I can do I will."

The Mark on my hand begins to crackle as I place it on her head.

Her hair rises like she's touching a Tesla coil.

The connection between us buzzes, humming along my skin, my whole arm going numb to the armpit. She makes a noise as I slide my magick into her goddess essence like a stiletto knife.

The moment I touch her . . . divinity? . . . power rushes out of her like a ruptured bladder, sweeping into me, and I drink, glory to goddess do I drink her down. The micromuscles in my body all convulse, contracting around the major ones as all of me suckles at all of Ashtoreth, the goddess of love.

I don't take it all.

But only because I can't hold it.

Time stretches around me, elastic in the moment, one second

of this exchange feeling like days spent in the heart of a nuclear reactor.

I pull my Mark off her in less time than it takes you to read this sentence.

She slumps, going boneless and limp as she kneels, crumpling to the floor.

She is not dead; she will recover from this; she is a goddess after all, even if she has fallen.

I feel like I could split the earth in two with the sheer force of my will.

I stand and look down at Ashtoreth, a red pinprick of place locked inside my mind. My super-charged magick wants to surge toward it, to pour into the collar and leap me there, but I hold it in check through sheer force of will, keeping my thoughts corralled in a straight line.

She looks up at me. She is dimmer. Diminished.

I say the only thing I can, the words firing down that straight line like bullets from the barrel of a pistol.

"Fucking die for all I care, Ashtoreth. We are through."

These are the last words I say to her before I wish myself away.

62

My feet hit the cobblestones and I can immediately feel the difference from earlier.

Everything feels . . . *spongier?*

Like it's made of sponge.

Carcosa has gone all squishy and porous.

And it's even darker, the not black of earlier now a pure ink.

The coat flares around me and I feel its anxiety against my skin.

The teleportation sucked up a lot of the magick I yanked out of Ashtoreth, but I still feel strong and ready, not sick and weak like I normally would. Before I move I do two things, kick my magick out to find the Man in Black and shake my hand to make the Mark on my palm flare so I can see.

Ashtoreth's energy has mixed with my magick and the colour of the light I cast is a pale violet. It flares out from my palm and lights up the cobblestones under my feet.

And reveals a trail of corpses.

The moment I see them I can smell them, a throat-closing bouquet of raw iron hemoglobin and the green stench of torn gut. There are tangles of legs under sections of white canvas stained with blood going rust coloured.

These were the followers of Hastur, the King in Yellow, the lunatics.

Slaughtered, no attempt made to hide them or to mask what has been done. The bodies look like they'd been hit by a train, all of them twisted together, some torn apart.

The Man in Black.

I begin moving, running as fast as I can with my hand held high to light the way, trying to not trip over the corpses under my feet.

63

I FIND THEM: Daniel, Javier, the skinhound, Mylendor, the Man in Black, and the King in Yellow—all in the same place.

Javier stands over Daniel holding one of the torches above them. He's got a hand on Daniel's chest, holding him on the bed. Daniel jerks around, struggling to get up. If he wasn't weak from being in a coma Javier wouldn't have stood a chance at holding him in place.

The skinhound stands in front of them, head down and hackles raised, a sound like a buzz saw grinding its way through a cinder block coming from his chest.

Mylendor crouches beside the skinhound, both hands gone that black basalt and her face a feral mask of eyes and teeth. Her lips are pulled back to her ears, mouth open to tear flesh.

In the middle of the cobblestones, ringed about with straitjacketed corpses, the Man in Black and the King in Yellow fight.

The King in Yellow has expanded, stretched long

and crooked, his wings fully out from under his robe. The segmented wings dart around his twisting body, their hard surfaces singing against each other as they block the blows from the Man in Black.

The Man in Black dances.

He is all violent poetry and savage grace as he capers around Hastur with Oathbreaker in his red right hand. The blackened blade licks out, slicing into the rainbow-sheened wings of Hastur and twisting with a flick of the Man in Black's wrist when it sinks deep. The motion causes that wing to snap and shred with a distorted screech like a broken guitar. He spins and twists, going up on his toes and arching his back and occasionally leaning in a way that human anatomy doesn't work like.

The King in Yellow is being whittled down, bit by bit.

He won't last much longer.

The Man in Black will win. I know this like I know my name is Charlotte Tristan Moore.

Like I know that we all die one day.

It strikes me like a fist. I've been played. This has all been a set up.

Hastur didn't control the Man in Black. The Man in Black controlled him. I've been bamboozled, hornswaggled, duped.

What the fuck else should I expect from a trickster god?

And now I know exactly what he has been doing this whole time.

He has two soul gems. He needs a third to free Azathoth from his prison, and when he kills the King in Yellow he will have it.

Unless . . .

I move toward the left, hand dropping into the pocket of the coat, fingers closing on the handle of the Aqedah.

"Charlie!"

I jump and wave for Javier to shut the fuck up.

"Ah, Thorn in My Pride!" The Man in Black smiles even as he lops off another three feet of Hastur's wing. "I see on your dumb human face that you now know what has happened right under your watchful gaze."

His arm moves, too quick for me to truly follow with my eyes, and the flat of Oathbreaker's blade slaps across the King in Yellow's face. I *feel* the noise of it in my chest more than hear it with my ears and Hastur drops to his knees.

The Man in Black slides behind him, black-bladed sword raised for a deathblow, and a smile of pure joy on his shark-toothed mouth.

"Wait!" My left hand flies up in a "Stop!" motion. "I have what you need; don't kill him."

Nyarlathotep cocks his head.

I reach in with my left hand and fish around in the left pocket of the coat. My hand swirls inside it, my fingers going numb with the cold. Nothing. I snap my fingers inside the depths of the coat, in the void that it holds, and the tips of them hurt they are so cold.

The coat babbles in my head.

Now.

The coat hisses at my command, but it shifts on my body, obeying, giving me what I want. Finally, it's there, the hard surface of it feeling slick under my numb, near frostbitten fingers.

I pull out the soul gem of Cthulhu and hold it up.

It's bigger than an ostrich egg, a shining crystal that pulses with energy, roiling from teal to putrid yellow to hot magenta. I don't study it, keeping my eyes on the chaos god in front of me. I don't want to see the tiny reflection of Cthulhu look at me with those big eyes, judging me for what I am doing.

I close my mind to the tiny voice of the old one that tries to reach me, to stop me.

"And here I thought I was the tricky one," the Man in Black says. "All this time and you had my brother's fetish hidden in my old slave." He shakes his head. "Tsk, tsk, tsk."

I step closer. "No need to kill Hastur. Take this one instead. You win."

His eyes narrow. "You surrender?"

"Charlie, what are you doing? Don't give *el Diablo* that thing!" Javier cries out. I glance over. He's holding Daniel now with both arms around his chest as Daniel struggles even more.

Is he trying to get to me or to the Man in Black?

"I know what I'm doing, Javi. Just hold him there."

The skinhound trots forward and I shake my head. He understands and moves back to beside Mylendor.

"Save Hastur and I am your servant," Mylendor calls to me. "Save my lover."

The Man in Black arches one satanic eyebrow. "My, my, such the offers to you, Charlotte Tristan Moore. Who knew you were so charismatic?"

"All I want is that ring."

"Of course you do," he says. "You are nothing if not tenacious. I would like an answer to something first."

"What?"

"If you trade that fetish for this bauble"—he raises his red right hand and the emerald ring flares in the low light, sparking as if it has electricity in it—"then I will travel to the stronghold where my father dwells and free him, giving him this world as a feast of celebration."

"That isn't a question."

"That was the preface." He smiles, tilting his head. "This is the inquiry: When this inevitable happenstance occurs your entire world will be destroyed; why not leave your paramour oblivious until then?"

"Because I miss him."

"You would trade your world for time with him?"

I let all of my weariness and frustration out in a long sigh. "I've been through too much shit not to at this point." I raise the soul gem. "Give me your word and I will take it. Ring for soul gem, even steven swapsies."

He studies me for a long moment before sheathing Oathbreaker in his belt, reaching over, and slipping the ring off his red right hand. "Even steven swapsies," he intones solemnly.

We move closer, like two blind dogs who smell the same marrowbone, both of us holding out the thing the other wants.

Close enough, we reach at the same time and I pluck the ring from his fingers the same time he takes the soul gem from mine.

I move back immediately, making distance.

The Man in Black looks down at me, brows knit together over deep cave eyes.

"What?" I say.

"I did not expect that to go as we agreed."

"I trusted you."

"Even after all the treachery?"

"*You* still don't lie."

"This is true."

I feel like I am far enough away. "You have your things; now piss off."

"You were my favorite Acolyte, Charlotte Tristan Moore."

"You were a shitty mentor."

"Now you are just being obstinate."

I shrug and make a shooing motion with my hands.

The Man in Black touches his brow with the fingertips of his red right hand in salute, a sly, shark-toothed smile on his mouth. "Fare thee well."

And like that, in a swirl of magick and brimstone, he is gone.

64

Daniel screams.

Javier lies across him as the bed rattles on the cobblestones. I move quickly, wrapping his flailing arm under mine and pulling his hand up. The ring slips over his finger like it wants to go there.

It seats against his knuckle with an audible *crack!* as the gem in it lights up like it has gone radioactive.

Daniel goes limp, every ounce of tension just gone.

Is he . . . ?

"Javier, move! Let me see!" I shove him off Daniel, searching with my eyes and feeling with my hands.

I almost fall to my knees with relief to find he is still breathing.

"It's okay, Charlie; it's cool," Javier says.

The ring begins to dim and the gold band melts, flowing into the skin on the back of Daniel's hand; the emerald stutters in and out of existence, each stutter sinking it a fraction into Daniel's fingers.

After a few minutes, it disappears.

Daniel lies on the bed. He looks as if he is just sleeping.

God, please let him just be sleeping.

Something bumps my hip and the coat trills in my head. I look down and the skinhound is there, looking up with his one eye tilted toward me.

I drop to a crouch and put my hands on the sides of his slick skull. I stroke him like a real dog, ignoring the feeling of my fingers skipping over little bunches of muscles, slipping through the viscous fluid that coats the skinhound from nose to tail. As I pet him I murmur to him, "Good boy. You guarded him, gooooood boy." His jaw full of bone-cracking teeth opens and his tongue lolls out as he begins panting.

He looks so much like a real dog it yanks a sharp laugh from me that hurts my chest when it comes.

"Hey, Charlie, where's Ash?"

The question makes me sigh. I try to keep my voice even, but there's an edge to it. "She's not coming."

Javier takes the news with a nod. "Is she . . . ?" He lets it trail off.

"No." *But she should be.*

"So—"

I cut him off. "If you ever see her again, run. Don't trust her."

Hands up. "Okay, okay, jeez."

I need to move.

Time is passing and I need to do what I need to do before I lose my nerve.

I do not want to do what I need to do.

Goddammit.

I give the skinhound a gentle push away and stand. Looking around, I find Mylendor crouched beside the King in Yellow. Walking over to them, my feet feel like they are encased in lead.

As I draw near, Mylendor looks at me warily.

"How is he?" I ask.

"Weak, but he is eternal; he will recover."

Hastur looks like a scarecrow made of sticks and burlap. His yellow robe is tattered, ragged, and torn, and most of his wings lie scattered in pieces on the ground around us. I squat down in front of him. His skin has gone from creamy jaundice to full neon daffodil, so yellow it nearly hurts to look at him. His lips tremble, pulled thin across his mouth, and his eyes are so sunken into his triangular skull that the lazy one doesn't even roll, just lies in its socket staring at me as if I'm not there.

"That true, Ramblin' Wreck? You still a god up in there?"

He tries to speak, his mouth moving but no sound coming. He shifts in Mylendor's arms and the one cicada wing chimes out all forlorn and empty. A tongue the colour of recycled paper licks his too-thin lips as he finds his voice. "Did you set her free?"

"Yeah, she's not held captive anymore."

His smile is weak but there. "Good. Well done, my good and faithful—"

"Stop," I say. "Your servant is the one holding you. I was your patsy."

"I had no choice. You should know that. He was my puppeteer."

"They were your strings to pull."

He nods assent.

"Do you still have that bracelet?"

He lifts his arm. There on his wrist dangles the bracelet. "It gave him enough control to defeat me."

"You two aren't equals," I say as I reach out and pull the bracelet off his arm and drop it into one of the coat's pockets. "If you were, he wouldn't have been able to control you at all."

"Equal enough that he would have left me be."

I stand; the coat helps. "Mylendor."

She purrs in response.

"You two are lovers?"

"Yesss," she hisses.

"Must suck to hear him still ask about the other woman."

"Doesn't matter. I am his. I would die for him, kill for him, love for him." Her wide eyes almost spin in their sockets.

"Do you remember your offer if I saved him?"

"That I would be your servant?"

"Yeah. Was that bullshit?"

"I meant it."

Here we go.

The coat burbles along the back of my skull.

"Hey, Hastur."

He looks up at me, leaning back on Mylendor. The dumb bitch wraps her arms around him even tighter and begins licking the side of his neck with a tongue too long to fit inside her mouth. "Yes?"

"If it were your free will, would you have done anything differently?"

It takes him a long moment to answer. "No, not for you."

"Thought so."

The coat flares out around me, opening across my chest as my hand sinks into its depths and comes out with Ephraim's shotgun. I can feel the heat of the hellfire in the chamber through the Mark on my hand as I pull it clear.

I drop the slide into my other hand and pull the trigger.

65

THE GOUT OF balefire obliterates both of their heads, just shears them off the necks underneath.

I rack the slide, then drop the shotgun back into the coat locked and loaded.

I hear Javier yelling something, but it's muffled and distant, my ears shut from the blast I just fired.

I'm ignoring him anyway, I have to do this before I change my mind.

The bodies slide sideways, still wrapped around each other. I drop to my knees beside them and the coat puts the Aqedah in my hand the second it slips into the pocket. A handful of that ratty yellow robe lets me pull Hastur's body closer.

The skinhound is there, across the body from me, watching as he noses the body of the dead god. Wisps of smoke come off the charred flesh at the stump of the neck. The skinhound licks it experimentally.

He whuffs and jumps back like a real dog with a snout full of pepper.

"Good boy," I say.

The Aqedah goes into Hastur's chest just as easy as it has gone into everything else. I pull it down, slicing hard, making a big opening. I push up the sleeve of the coat, take a deep breath, and shove my hand inside.

It's like shoving my hand in a deep vat of moist compost.

There isn't any structure; it's just mealy, mushy stuff that feels like dirt. Occasionally there is a hard spot that brushes against my arm, but mostly it's just cool moistness.

Come on. You all have one.

The side of my hand knocks against something hard and round.

Gotcha.

The thing rolls over my wrist when I try to grab it, swinging like a pendulum. It takes a few grabs to get it. Once I do I drag it out.

As the stuff inside Hastur that coats my arm hits the air it liquifies and runs rivulets down my arm.

Ugh.

The thing I pull out is a white sphere. Thin lines, like hairline cracks, swirl around the surface. I feel it pulse in my hand, laden with a slow thudding power.

The soul gem of the King in Yellow.

"Charlie."

It's Javier's voice.

"Charlie, he's awake."

Wait.

Daniel.

I pocket the soul gem and stand, shaking the ichor of Hastur (say that three times fast) off my arm. The skinhound bumps me before I can take a step.

I push back with my thigh and he bumps me harder.

I look down at him.

The coat sings and I get it.

"You're with me?" I ask the vivisected canine by my side.

He answers with a yip.

All right then.

I move over to Javier and Daniel, who is sitting up on the bed now. He's thin, so thin, compared to how he looked before, but his eyes are bright and clear.

"Hey, Charlie," he says. Damn, his little crooked smile gets me.

"Hey."

He moves his head, looking around pointedly. "Seems like some weird shit has happened."

"More than I'd like."

He nods and his bangs fall over his eyes. He blows them up out of the way. "You look good."

"Baby"—it feels right calling him that—"I look terrible."

"Well, yeah, but it seems like a million years since I've seen you."

"You've been away for a while."

"Not a million years, I hope."

"No, not that long."

"Good." He smiles a little again and takes a deep breath. "I'm still pretty tired."

"You can rest." Oh god. "Javier will watch over you."

"Javier?" he asks.

Javier moves around beside me. "Hey, Daniel."

"Hey. Okay." He squints at Javier. "I don't know you, do I?"

"No, *esse,* but we cool."

Daniel looks at me.

"You two are cool," I assure him.

Daniel nods. "Solid."

I take a deep breath. This is hard. Getting harder.

"You did it," Daniel says.

"Did what?"

"Won."

Fuck.

He looks at my face. "What is it?"

"I have to go."

"It's not over?"

"No." *Not by a long shot.*

He pushes to stand. The bed rolls a little and Javier catches it before it gets away. The movement makes Daniel's hospital gown rise and I look up at his eyes before it gets too high.

I'm not ready for anything like that.

And I have to go.

"Daniel . . ."

"Let's go," he says.

"You can't. I'm sending you with Javier."

"Dammit, Charlie," he says.

I put my hand on his chest and he stops. I reach over and touch Javier on his arm.

"I love you, Daniel; that's why I have to try and stop him."

"Let me . . ."

"Javier, take care of him."

"Okay, *chica.*" Javier grins.

Daniel grabs the coat. Tears roll down his face. "Charlie, I love you; I just got you back; don't do this."

"I love you." Over my shoulder I say to the skinhound, "Stay." *Now.*

The coat furls around the three of us, wrapping us tightly as I pick my place and wish. The remnants of Ashtoreth's essence bubble up from inside me and we slide sideways across space, protected by the coat.

The moment we hit linoleum the coat opens and I smell that hospital smell. The room looks the same and it's empty, which is good. Daniel and Javier stagger a few steps away as the coat opens. Daniel turns, looking at me with an expression that cuts me to the core.

"Don't go," he says.

I take one last long look at him, memorizing every detail that I can, as the coat closes around me. One wish and I'm moving back to Carcosa.

The skinhound waits where I left him.

"Ready to go?" I ask him.

He bounces his skull up and down in what looks like a nod. I crouch, draping the coat over him and pulling him close. My chest is tight, but I keep moving, keep working, to keep from crying.

The bracelet that was on Hastur's wrist is in my right hand. I spit on the Mark there, the body fluid really kicking the magick into gear. The torc tightens around my throat as I trace the Man in Black, the one who owned this jewelry he used to control Hastur. The line stretches far, far away, pulled as thin as a strand of spider silk.

But it is still attached.

I find him, a crimson pinprick on the velvet of the universe.

The coat singsongs around it.

Yes, it's a long way. You can stay; you don't have to go; just give me my weapons.

The song in my brain turns harsh, scouring around the edges of my brainpan, and I hear that it won't abandon me.

And fuck me for thinking it would.

Okay, okay, sheesh.

I reach in and take hold of the Hastur gem, letting its smooth surface fill my palm. The power in it throbs, making the bones of my wrist ache.

I hope it's enough as I fixate on the Man in Black and make my wish.

If not we will be stranded somewhere in the middle of the universe.

I take a deep breath and begin to draw in the power of the gem, making my magick go bubbly and acidic in my veins.

Get ready you red-handed son of a bitch, 'cause here I come.

ABOUT THE AUTHOR

LEVI BLACK lives in Metro Atlanta with his wife and an array of toys, books, records, and comics. He's been weird his whole life and is almost as scary as he looks. Visit him at https://leviblackbooks.wordpress.com.